Malorie Blackman

Whizziwig
Returns

Illustrated by Stephen Lee

PUFFIN BOOKS

For Neil and Elizabeth, with love

PUFFIN BOOKS

Published by the Penguin Group
Penguin Books Ltd, 27 Wrights Lane, London W8 5TZ, England
Penguin Putnam Inc., 375 Hudson Street, New York, New York 10014, USA
Penguin Books Australia Ltd, Ringwood, Victoria, Australia
Penguin Books Canada Ltd, 10 Alcorn Avenue, Toronto, Ontario, Canada M4V 3B2
Penguin Books (NZ) Ltd, Private Bag 102902, NSMC, Auckland, New Zealand

Penguin Books Ltd, Registered Offices: Harmondsworth, Middlesex, England

First published 1999
1 3 5 7 9 10 8 6 4 2

Puffin Film and TV Tie-in edition first published 1999

Text copyright © Oneta Malorie Blackman, 1999
Illustrations copyright © Stephen Lee, 1999
All rights reserved

The moral right of the author and illustrator has been asserted

Set in Baskerville

Made and printed in England by Clays Ltd, St Ives plc

British Library Cataloguing in Publication Data
A CIP catalogue record for this book is available from the British Library

ISBN 0-141-30458-8

PUFFIN BOOKS

Whizziwig Returns

'What's going on? HELP!' Steve cried out.

Ben stared. 'Steve, what're you . . . Whizziwig!'

'You did wish Steve was a bit lighter,' Whizziwig reminded him.

'I didn't mean for you to turn him into a helium balloon.' Ben shook his head.

'Argue about it later. Get me down.' Steve's head hit the ceiling. 'Ouch!'

Whizziwig floated up to Steve's eye level. 'It's good up here, isn't it? You get a great view of the whole room. And you just wait until you see –'

'Get me down – NOW!' Steve roared.

Ben pulled at Steve's legs. Steve came down all right, but then Ben had to keep pressing on his shoulders to keep him on the ground.

'Whizziwig, change me back.'

'Sorry. You know the rules.' Whizziwig shrugged.

Contents

Chapter One

Tap! Tap! Tap!

Tap! Tap! Tap! Ben sat up abruptly. Tap! Tap! There it was again. Someone was knocking at the window. But that couldn't be right . . . His bedroom was up on the first floor of the house. Tap! Ben switched on his bedside lamp. Should he go and get his mum and dad? Tappity-tap!

'Ben! Aren't you going to let me in?'

He recognized that voice at once. 'WHIZZIWIG!'

Ben rushed to the window and threw back the curtains. And there she was, hovering just outside his window. Ben flung it wide open. In the moonlight as well as the light given off by his bedside lamp, Whizziwig sparkled with gold and silver and rainbow colours – at least, that's how it seemed to Ben. She floated into the room, a beaming smile on her face.

'Whizziwig! How are you? I've really missed you. Things have been so dull around here since you left! Apart from with Mrs Leonard! She still claps her hands over her mouth in mid-sentence! And Splitter was a bit more human for a while, but he's back to his normal self now. And –'

'Goodness me!' Whizziwig put her hand over Ben's mouth. 'Could I possibly get two words in edgeways!'

Ben grinned. 'I'm just so happy to see you. Where's your spaceship?'

'Up on your roof. I hope that's OK?'

''Course it is.'

Ben climbed back into bed while Whizziwig floated around the room. He couldn't stop grinning. This reminded him of when he'd first met Whizziwig. She'd scared the life out of him then – until he'd got to know her.

'So how was your trip? How was your aunt?'

Whizziwig had left Earth the last time to go and visit her auntie.

'She's fine. I told her all about my adventures on this planet. She laughed her fur off!' Whizziwig smiled.

'Does your aunt look like you?'

'A bit. I got all the good looks in the family though,' Whizziwig said modestly.

Ben wasn't quite sure what to say to that! 'Good-looking' wasn't exactly the first phrase that popped into his head whenever he saw Whizziwig. He wondered what Whizziwig's aunt looked like. How he would love to meet her and the rest of Whizziwig's family.

'Whizzy, d'you think that maybe one day we could –'

'Ben, are you awake in there?'

'Quick! Hide!' Ben urged.

Whizziwig flew to the top of the wardrobe in a flash, just as Dad came into the room.

'Ben, are you OK? Did you have a nightmare?'

'Er, no . . . I mean, yes . . . I mean . . .' Ben did his best not to look directly at Whizziwig, who was bobbing up and down behind his dad's head. 'I mean, I'm fine now.'

'You're sure?'

'Yes.'

'Then get some sleep. It's very late.'

'OK, Dad.'

Dad left the room, quietly shutting the door behind him. Ben waited a moment before beckoning to Whizziwig.

'It's OK. You can come down now.'

Whizziwig floated towards him.

'Just like old times!' Ben sighed happily. 'I know Steve will be glad to see you.'

'Excellent!' said Whizziwig. 'I still have a lot to learn from your planet. That's why I came back. I've been asked to write a report about life on Earth. Tomorrow I shall help you at school and begin my observations.'

Oh-oh! Ben didn't like the sound of that. He remembered the chaos Whizziwig inevitably caused whenever she 'helped' out in any way. She granted only unselfish wishes made for someone else. It was funny how much trouble unselfish wishes could cause. Like when she'd

4

granted Charlotte's wish that Ben would kiss her every time he looked at her and he'd got into real trouble with Mr Archer because of it. Or the time she'd filled his garden with bikes and Mum was trapped. Or the time she turned Splitter, the school bully, into a donkey – mind you, that was funny!

'Now, if you don't mind,' said Whizziwig, 'I've had a very long journey so I think I'll shut down and recharge my primary energy. My secondary energy could do with a top-up as well.'

'Oh, OK,' said Ben.

Whizziwig ducked under Ben's bed and said with a yawn, 'Good night, Ben.'

'Good night, Whizziwig.'

Ben switched off his bedside lamp and lay in the dark for a while. To be honest, he was a bit worried about what was going to happen tomorrow with Whizziwig around. But nothing much could go wrong if she just watched from his bag – could it?

Ben closed his eyes and drifted off to sleep, telling himself that everything would be fine. But there was a part of him that wasn't so sure . . .

Chapter Two

One of
Those Days

It was Thursday morning and Ben was having breakfast. He ate his bacon and beans on toast in silence while he listened to Mum and Dad argue.

'I can't believe you, Daniel. We've had today planned for weeks.' Mum was not at all happy.

'I know, darling, but everything – and I mean *everything* – went wrong yesterday. The building materials for stage two still haven't arrived, the site foreman broke his leg and my plans for this month's work have gone missing. If I'm not there today to supervise, things will go from bad to worse.'

'Can't you get someone else to handle it?' asked Mum.

'It's my project, babe. I've got to be there to sort things out,' Dad soothed.

The doorbell rang.

'I'll get it.' Ben leapt to his feet.

As he left the kitchen, he saw Whizziwig floating in the hall just below the ceiling. 'Whizziwig, you can't stay there. Someone will see you.'

'No chance. I can duck.' Whizziwig zipped to one side of the doorframe. 'I can dodge.' Whizziwig zipped to the other side. 'I can weave –'

'Yeah! Yeah! Just stay out of sight,' Ben pleaded.

'Don't I always?' Whizziwig smiled.

Ben opened the front door. It was Steve.

'Hi! D'you want some breakfast?' Ben asked.

'Wouldn't say no.' Steve licked his lips.

They made their way to the kitchen.

'Hi, Whizzy,' Steve grinned. 'Welcome back!'

'You saw me then?' Whizziwig said, surprised.

Ben gave Whizziwig an 'I told you so!' look.

''Course I saw you. Why? Are you meant to be invisible or something?' asked Steve.

'Or something!' Ben answered before Whizziwig could.

As they walked into the kitchen, Mum and Dad were still arguing.

'I had it all arranged,' said Mum. 'Aunt Dottie has Lizzie, and Ben was going there straight after school, and you and I –'

'Sorry, love. Can't be helped.' Dad glanced down at his watch. 'I've got to go.'

'I'm beginning to wonder if you wanted to take this day off in the first place.' Mum's eyes narrowed.

'How can you say that?' Dad exclaimed. 'I wish you could've had a day like I had yesterday. I'm telling you, *everything* went wrong.'

Ben and Steve exchanged a worried look before both glancing out of the kitchen door. Whizziwig was hanging upside down from the top of the doorframe like a furry bat and she had a huge grin on her face.

'I don't think I'll bother with breakfast,' Steve said hastily. 'Maybe we should just go.'

'Don't mind me, Steve.' Mum shook her head. 'I'm a bit disappointed, that's all.'

Dad gave Mum a quick kiss before he rushed out of the room and out of the house. Mum sighed deeply and picked up her coffee cup to take a sip. Somehow the coffee missed her mouth and spilt down the front of her shirt. Ben decided it was definitely time to go before things got any worse.

'Bye, Mum,' said Ben.

And giving Mum no time to say another word, he and Steve raced out of the kitchen and up the stairs to Ben's room.

'D'you think we should warn her that she might be in for a bad day?' Ben asked, flopping down on his bed.

'She wouldn't believe you, not without proof,' said Steve, looking straight at Whizziwig.

Whizziwig took one look at Steve's face and floated out of harm's way. 'My! That's an interesting bit of the ceiling!' she said.

Steve and Ben smiled. It made a change to

wind up Whizziwig, rather than the other way around.

'So, did you finish your science project then?' Steve asked.

'Almost! D'you want to see? It's up there on top of my wardrobe.'

'Why did you put it up there?' Steve frowned.

'So Tarzan couldn't get at it, of course,' Ben replied. Tarzan was their large black and white Collie dog. 'Dad put it up there for me. Help me get it down.'

Steve and Ben walked over to the wardrobe.

'I'll lift you up,' said Ben.

Huffing and puffing, Ben held on to Steve's legs and hoisted him up.

Steve stretched out a hand towards Ben's science project but he couldn't quite reach.

'A little higher,' Steve said.

'Hurry up, Steve. You're breaking my back.'

'Don't drop me,' Steve ordered. 'Almost got it –'

'Steve . . . Ouch! Hurry . . . up . . . Ooh, I wish you were a bit lighter. My arms are killing me.'

Whizziwig's eyes sparkled. The wish was granted. Only neither Ben nor Steve realized what had just happened. Steve managed to get the board with Ben's weather-station science project off the top of the wardrobe.

'Oh, that's better,' said Ben, surprised. It no longer felt like he was lifting up a baby elephant!

Ben let Steve down and took the weather-station off him to make sure it was still OK. Immediately, Steve started to float up to the ceiling.

'What's going on? HELP!' Steve cried out.

Ben stared. 'Steve, what're you . . . Whizziwig!'

'You did wish Steve was a bit lighter,' Whizziwig reminded him.

'I didn't mean for you to turn him into a helium balloon.' Ben shook his head.

'Argue about it later. Get me down.' Steve's head hit the ceiling. 'Ouch!'

Whizziwig floated up to Steve's eye level. 'It's good up here, isn't it? You get a great view of the whole room. And you just wait until you see –'

'Get me down – NOW!' Steve roared.

Ben pulled at Steve's legs. Steve came down all right, but then Ben had to keep pressing on his shoulders to keep him on the ground.

'Whizziwig, change me back.'

'Sorry. You know the rules.' Whizziwig shrugged.

'But . . . but I can't go to school like this.'

'School!' Ben exclaimed. 'We'd better hurry up or we'll be late.'

Ben let go of Steve and ran over to his bookcase to get his school books. Steve started to float up to the ceiling again. Ben grabbed him and pulled him down.

'What am I supposed to do?' Steve asked.

Ben looked around his room. 'Wait here.'

Ben ran downstairs as Steve floated upwards. Steve put out his hands to try to stop his head banging into the lampshade in the middle of the room. And all the time he scowled at Whizziwig.

'If looks could kill, I'd be in serious trouble!' Whizziwig muttered.

Ben ran into the kitchen and started rummaging through one of the cupboards.

'Ben, what're you looking for?' said Mum.

'Er . . . something heavy,' Ben replied.

'Pardon?'

Ben took out as many tin cans and full jars as he could carry.

'Where d'you think you're going with all those?' frowned Mum.

'I . . . er, I need them for the school's Harvest Festival.'

'In spring?'

'Mr Archer wants us to rehearse as much as possible before autumn. Bye.' Ben tried to rush out of the kitchen before his mum could ask any more awkward questions.

'Hang on, Ben. You can't take all that stuff.'

'Please, Mum. You'll get it back tomorrow – I promise.'

'Oh, all right then,' Mum grumbled. 'Let me help you.'

'No! It's OK. Steve and I can manage.' Ben raced out of the room.

'What d'you mean "manage"?' Mum started to go after Ben, but she stubbed her toe on a chair leg. 'Ow! Ouch!' Hopping around in agony, Mum bumped into the table. Ben's half-full glass of milk fell off the table and on to the floor with a CRAA-AAA-AASH!

Ben strode rather than ran up the stairs because he didn't want to drop any cans or jars on his feet. By the time he got back to his bedroom, Steve's whole body was floating prone against the ceiling.

'Get me down,' Steve yelled.

'Shush! Hang on.'

Ben dumped all the cans and jars in his arms

on his bed. Then he ran downstairs again. He went into the kitchen to get a broom out of the cupboard before racing off again. Mum was under the table, carefully picking up the bits of broken glass.

'Ben . . .' Mum raised her head, only to bang it on the underside of the table. 'Ouch!'

'Can't stop, Mum. Bye.' Ben rushed out.

In his bedroom, Ben used the brush end to hook Steve's arm and pull him down.

'Ouch! Watch what you're doing!' Steve said angrily when Ben hit him on the head with the broom.

'That's a strange way to brush his hair!' said Whizziwig.

'I'm trying to get him down,' Ben said.

'How? By knocking my head off?' Steve snapped.

'Then try grabbing for the broom instead of letting me do all the work.' Ben was beginning to lose patience now.

Steve managed to reach the broom and Ben pulled him down.

'Hold on to my headboard or the wardrobe door while I sort out these cans,' said Ben.

Steve held on to the wardrobe door, his feet

floating behind and above him so that he looked like he was about to dive into the wardrobe. Ben emptied all of Steve's stuff out on to his bed, then filled his bag with the cans and jars. He topped it up with a couple of thick encyclopedias.

'There! That ought to do it!' Ben helped Steve to put his bag back on.

'It weighs a ton,' Steve complained.

'That's the whole idea,' Ben pointed out. 'Try walking.'

Steve let go of the wardrobe very, very carefully. He didn't float! He didn't rise! Ben beamed at him. Steve tried to walk. It was a bit loppity, a cross between how a kangaroo and a rabbit might walk, but at least he was down on the ground.

'Come on, Steve. We'd better get to school.'

'This should be interesting!' Whizziwig grinned.

Chapter Three

One of Those Days for Mum

Mum had all the broken pieces of glass in the dustpan. Now she needed some newspaper to wrap them in before she put them in the bin. Where had Daniel put all the old newspapers? Mum opened the cupboard over the sink. Ah! There were some newspapers –

right up on the top shelf! It was a bit of a stretch, but if she stood on tiptoe . . .

Mum reached up to pull the newspapers from above her head. They were a bit reluctant to move. She pulled harder. They still didn't budge.

'Why on earth did he put them up there?' Mum said crossly. She pulled harder still. Suddenly the newspapers shifted. Unfortunately, they weren't the only things to shift. Ben's dad had put a number of small pots of paint on top of the newspapers and they all came tumbling down on top of Mum. They were small enough not to hurt too much, but that didn't stop the lids flying off in all directions. Forest-green, midnight-blue and sunshine-yellow paints rained down. Mum's face, her hair, her clothes, they were all covered.

'ARGGHHH!' Mum let out a shriek and tried to duck out of the way – but she was too late.

She stood in the kitchen, snorting with rage like a demented bull.

'Daniel . . .' Laser beams shot out of Mum's eyes. Ben's dad would never know how lucky he was not to be in the house at that precise moment. 'DANIEL!' Mum stamped her foot.

She wiped the paint off her eyelids and from around her mouth. She'd have more than one or two choice words to say to Dad when he got home, that was for sure.

Chapter Four

One of Those
Days for Steve

Steve and Ben walked to school together, but Steve wasn't happy.

'This doesn't feel right. It's like I'm about to float off at any second,' said Steve.

'You mustn't,' Ben said, panicking. 'Outside

there's nothing to stop you floating up and up and up.'

'Then do something.' Steve frowned. 'Hold my hand or something.'

'Are you nuts? I'm not walking to school holding your hand! Suppose someone sees us?'

'I didn't mean it like that,' Steve said impatiently. 'I meant hold on to my arm or my shoulder.'

'I'm not sure about that either,' Ben said doubtfully.

'Then think of something – fast.'

Just then they saw a girl of about five or six standing in her front garden under a tree. She was crying her eyes out.

'Are you OK? What's the matter?' Ben asked.

The girl pointed up. 'My cat's stuck in that tree.'

'I'll get it down,' Steve said at once.

He shrugged his rucksack carefully off his back, letting it drop to the pavement. Immediately he began to float upwards. As he grabbed hold of the lower branches of the tree, the cat took one look at him, snarled and spat in fright, before scarpering down as fast as it could.

'Steve, you moron. You got the cat down, but who's going to get you down?' asked Ben.

'Wow!' The girl stared at Steve. 'Superboy!'

Whizziwig popped up from Ben's bag. 'What's happening?' She glanced up at Steve. 'That's very brave, Steve. Stupid but brave!'

'Wow!' The girl stared at Whizziwig. 'Are you from Krypton too?'

'No. I'm from Oricon.' Whizziwig smiled.

Ben pulled off his jacket and threw one end of it up towards the tree branches. 'Steve, grab hold.'

'I'm trying.'

'You can say that again!' Ben said crossly.

Ben threw up his jacket again and this time Steve managed to get hold of the sleeve. Ben pulled him back down to the ground like reeling in a weightless fish. The girl ran up the path to her open front door.

'Mum! Mum!'

'Let's go!' Ben said quickly.

Whizziwig ducked back down into Ben's bag. Ben helped to put Steve's rucksack on his back.

They set off just as the girl's mum came running.

'Mum, Superboy got Ginger down from the

tree,' the girl told her mum. 'Look! Over there! Superboy! He can fly!'

'I think you've been watching too much telly.' The girl's mum frowned. 'Come into the house.'

'But . . .'

And the girl was ushered back into the house, with her mum shutting the door firmly behind her.

'Phew!' Ben breathed a sigh of relief. 'That was a bit too close.'

Chapter Five

Bad to Worse

Mum stepped into her bath and breathed a huge sigh of contentment. After practically scrubbing her skin off in the shower to get rid of all the paint, it was lovely just to relax in a warm bath. Mum leaned back and closed her eyes. As soon as she'd had a long soak, she'd go and pick up Lizzie from Aunt

Dottie. But for now she had at least an hour to herself. Delightful!

Ding-dong! Oh, no! She couldn't believe it! The doorbell! Ding-dong! There it was again. With an expression like a bulldog chewing a wasp, Mum stood up and stepped out of the bath. She put on her dressing gown and slippers and marched downstairs. She flung the door open, but to her surprise there was no one there.

'Hello?' Mum stared all around. She took a couple of steps down the garden path to take a look up and down the street. 'Hello?'

'Oh, hello, Mrs! I'm here to make your day. I've got mops, brushes, cloths . . .'

Mum glared at the tall, gangly man with a pencil-thin moustache who appeared from around next-door's hedge. With a huge, cheesy smile, he moved to stand just outside her gate.

'No, thank you. I don't want any.'

'But they're all good quality, top of the range –'

'No, thank you,' Mum said firmly. She was very aware that bathwater was running down her shins and calves and that her slippers were getting soggier by the second.

'Well, if you're sure I can't persuade you?' the salesman tried one last time.

'You can't. Goodbye,' Mum said.

The man walked off to try further up the road. Mum turned to go back into the house, but just at that moment the wind caught the door. She dived for the door but she was too late. It slammed shut just as she had her fingers on it.

'No!' Mum battered against the door with her fists. 'No! No! NO!' Then she leaned her head against it. Now what was she going to do? She scowled at the closed front door, willing it to open. But of course it didn't. And the back door was locked too. There was only one thing for it. She'd have to walk to the nearest phone box and call Daniel on his mobile phone. Then he could come home and let her in. Pulling her dressing gown more tightly around her, she set off down the road. She could only hope and pray that she didn't meet anyone she knew.

After ducking down in someone's front garden and hiding behind a letter box and two trees to make sure she wasn't seen, Mum finally made it to the nearest phone box. She dialled Daniel's mobile, but it just kept ringing.

'Come on, Daniel,' Mum muttered.

There was no answer And now an elderly woman was standing outside the phone box waiting to use it. And she was giving Mum a very peculiar look as she waited. Mum put the phone down and tried again, in case she'd dialled the wrong number. No luck. It still kept ringing. And now a young man and a teenage girl had joined the queue outside. Mum's whole body was on fire with embarrassment. Heaven only knew what they thought of her, standing in the phone box in her dressing gown and slippers and muttering to herself.

Mum came out, doing her best not to catch anyone's eye. What was she going to do now? There was only one answer. She'd have to get Ben's front-door key – which meant walking all the way to his school. She didn't fancy that idea at all, but she had no choice. At least she could cut through the park. That should be less embarrassing than walking along the main road.

Mum slunk along in the shadows, hiding behind cars and even behind a lamppost when she thought she spotted someone she knew. When at last she *did* reach the park, she breathed a huge sigh of relief. She ran in and darted from tree to tree like an overgrown squirrel. No way was she going to be seen. Now, if she could just make it around the pond and the children's playground to the opposite exit, then she'd –

'Gina? Gina, is that you?'

Mum recognized that voice at once. She didn't need to turn around to know that it was her friend, Ramona. Instantly, she legged it in the opposite direction. If Ramona realized that it was definitely her, then Mum knew she'd never hear the end of it. And she'd never live it down! Minutes later, she was well hidden behind the broad trunk of an old oak tree. Panting for breath, she risked a quick peek out from behind the trunk. She immediately ducked back again. Ramona and her grey poodle were heading in her direction, and they were getting closer and closer. Mum looked around frantically. The bushes by the pond – they were her only hope! She ran for them, trying to use the tree trunks to keep her out of Ramona's sight. Finally she made it, squatting down behind the bushes, hardly daring to breathe. A duck waddled up on to the narrow bank beside

Mum and, fixing her with a 'that's my spot!' stare, quacked and quacked.

'Shush!' Mum begged the duck.

'Isn't that bizarre, Gertie?' Mum heard Ramona say to her poodle. 'I could've sworn I saw Gina . . . But it couldn't have been. I mean, what would she be doing in the park in her dressing gown. It must've been someone else.'

'Woo-oo-oof!' Gertie replied.

'Let's get you home and I'll treat you to a delicious snack,' Ramona said, picking up her tiny dog.

Relieved, Mum watched as Ramona walked away, Gertie in her arms. At last things were starting to go right. Mum tried to stand up but there was something suspiciously slippery under her feet. Arms spinning like a windmill, she tried to steady herself, but it was no good. SPLASH! Mum fell into the duck pond and found herself sitting up to her waist in scummy water. The ducks around her swam away, quacking indignantly And as for Mum – her face was a picture, but not a pretty one!

Chapter Six

The Quarrel

Ben helped Steve to pull his heavy bag past his knees to stop him floating up in the classroom.

'The strap is really cutting into my legs,' Steve grumbled.

'It's this or float out of the window,' Ben told him.

'This is all your fault, Ben. How am I meant to go home like this?'

'My fault?' Ben stared. 'I like that!'

'Well, I'm glad one of us does,' Steve said bitterly.

'Don't start arguing, you two,' Whizziwig said from inside Ben's bag. 'Steve, I've been thinking, and this will cheer you up. How would you like to go for a fly around after school?'

'I can't fly. I just float – remember,' said Steve. He was still darting angry glances in Ben's direction.

'Yes, but how about if I attach a string to your hand and, as long as I don't let you go, you can fly around with me. Believe me, you'll see a lot of the world that way.' Whizziwig smiled.

'Well . . . I don't know . . .' Steve was obviously tempted.

Ben looked from Whizziwig to Steve and back again. 'But, Whizziwig, suppose you let go of the string? How would we ever get him down? No. He's not going to do it. It's too dangerous.'

'Ben, you're not my boss,' Steve said furiously. 'OK, Whizziwig! We'll go flying tonight after I've had my tea – all right?'

'Don't be stupid,' said Ben.

'Who're you calling stupid? I've had just about enough of you, Ben Sinclair.'

'OK, Tinker Bell! Keep your hair on!' Ben sniffed.

'Oh dear!' Whizziwig sighed, wondering what she'd started.

Mr Archer entered the room.

'You just wait,' Steve hissed.

'For what? For you to grow a brain? I won't live that long,' Ben hissed back.

'OK, everyone. Settle down,' Mr Archer called out.

Steve and Ben pulled their chairs away from each other and turned so that they were facing in opposite directions.

'Me and my big mouth!' Whizziwig muttered.

Mr Archer started talking about shapes and angles, and still Ben and Steve wouldn't talk to each other. Until at last, Ben couldn't stand it any longer.

'I can't believe you'd risk floating off into space just to spite me,' Ben hissed.

'It's not to spite you. The whole world doesn't revolve around you, you know.'

'Look, you –' Ben turned, angry.

'Steve, could you come up here and fill in one of these missing answers please?' called out Mr Archer.

'Sir?'

'Up here – missing angles – fill in please,' Mr Archer drawled.

Steve stared helplessly at his teacher. Ben stared helplessly at Steve. If he budged a centimetre off the chair without his bag, he would float off and then what would Mr Archer say?

'Sometime before I draw my pension would be nice,' Mr Archer said with sarcasm.

'I can't, sir.'

'Why not?'

'I can't move. My legs – my whole body –' Steve stammered.

'I'll do it, sir,' Ben volunteered.

'I asked Steve, not you.' Mr Archer frowned. 'And why the sudden enthusiasm? Usually I have to practically drag you up here! Now come on, Steve. I haven't got all day.'

Ben stared at the questions on the board. He was going to have to work *fast*.

'Sir, the first angle is forty-five degrees, the

second one is ninety and the third one is sixty,'
Ben called out.

'Ben!' Mr Archer was astounded – and he
wasn't the only one. Everyone in the class was
staring at him! 'As you're so keen, maybe you'd
like more homework. I'm obviously not
stretching you enough.'

'I'm being stretched, sir – honest,' Ben said
hastily.

'Hmmm! Well, your answers are absolutely
right, so well done – but don't call them out like
that in future,' said Mr Archer.

'Don't worry. It won't happen again!' Ben
had a headache from having to work out the
answers so fast. He wasn't going to do that again
in a hurry.

'OK, everyone. Let's look at the first triangle.'
Mr Archer turned back to the board.

'Thanks, Ben,' Steve whispered.

'You're welcome,' Ben replied softly.

Ben and Steve exchanged a smile and, just
like that, they were friends again.

Without warning, the door flew open.
Everyone looked around at once. In walked
Ben's mum in her dressing gown and slippers.
And she was dripping wet.

'Excuse me, Mr Archer,' Mum said.

Mr Archer stared at her, stunned. Mum made her way over to Ben's table.

'Ben, can I have your front-door key please? I've locked myself out,' she said.

Ben stood up slowly, staring at his mum as if he'd never seen her before. He fished his key out of his pocket and handed it over, never taking his eyes off her.

'Thanks, Ben. I'll see you later.' Mum turned and walked back to the door. 'Sorry to interrupt your lesson, Mr Archer.'

'Not at all, Mrs Sinclair.' Mr Archer was still staring.

Mum strode out of the room, shutting the door carefully behind her.

Ben sat down. All eyes were upon him.

'OK! OK! Back to work, you lot. The excitement's over.' Mr Archer was the first to recover.

'What was that all about?' Steve whispered.

'No idea.' Ben shrugged. His eyes suddenly narrowed. 'Whizziwig, this wouldn't have anything to do with you and that wish Dad made this morning, would it?'

'Why do I get blamed for everything?' Whizziwig said crossly.

'Shush!' Ben urged. 'And there's no need to get your fur in a knot! I was only asking.'

As Ben straightened up, he wasn't entirely convinced, however, that Whizziwig didn't have a hand in Mum's sudden appearance. Whenever something bizarre happened, she was usually behind it.

Chapter Seven

The PE Lesson

When Ben and Steve left the canteen after lunch, neither of them said a word. Ben because he thought he shouldn't and Steve because he couldn't. Wearing his rucksack all the way through lunch had given him backache and carrying it around all the time was wearing him out. They both made their way back to the classroom, where Steve slid his bag down his back and wrapped it round his legs before he sank into his chair.

'Almost home-time.' Ben tried to cheer up Steve. 'Lunch is over and done with and this afternoon shouldn't be too bad.'

'Why not?'

'That theatre group is coming in for the afternoon remember?' said Ben. 'And once they've finished, it'll be home-time.'

The school buzzer sounded. Mr Archer was in the classroom before it had finished making a racket throughout the school. The rest of the class trooped in, chatting and laughing.

'I have an announcement to ... THAT'S QUITE ENOUGH NOISE PLEASE!' Mr Archer shouted above the din. 'Thank you. Now, as I was saying, I have an announcement to make. I'm afraid I have some bad news. The theatre group who were supposed to visit us this afternoon have had to cancel.'

The whole class groaned.

'So we can all do some extra maths or we can have a PE lesson,' said Mr Archer. 'Which one is it?'

'PE! PE!' most of the class shouted.

'Maths! Maths!' yelled Steve and Ben.

Everyone else – including Mr Archer – looked at Ben and Steve as if they were seriously nutty!

'I'm afraid you two are outvoted,' Mr Archer said. 'OK, everyone, gather up your things and let's go to the changing rooms.'

'Sir, couldn't Steve and I stay here and do some extra maths?' Ben pleaded.

'We wouldn't mind – honest,' Steve added.

'Well, I do. We're all going out to get some exercise – and that means you two as well. Up and at 'em!'

Ben and Steve dragged their feet all the way to the boys' changing rooms, but they still got there.

'What am I going to do?' Steve asked.

'My mind has gone blank,' Ben admitted. He whispered into his bag, 'Whizziwig, I don't suppose you have any ideas?'

'I'm afraid my head is empty too,' said Whizziwig.

'I never said . . . never mind.' Ben decided against trying to explain what he meant.

Mr Archer came into the changing rooms to usher the boys out. 'Steve, why haven't you got changed yet?'

'Er . . . Mr Archer, I was thinking . . . I was thinking I might like to join the SAS when I leave school,' Steve began.

'Oh, yes?' Mr Archer raised an eyebrow.

'And they have to run for ages wearing heavy backpacks to build up their strength and their stamina and their muscles. So I was wondering if I . . .' Steve looked at Ben. 'I mean, if *we* could go running with our backpacks on?'

'Running? I thought we could all have a game of football or rounders,' said Mr Archer. 'You really want to run?'

'Yes, please. Don't we, Ben?'

The very last thing in the world Ben wanted to do was go running with a heavy backpack on, but what could he say?

'Yes, sir,' Ben replied reluctantly.

'Suit yourselves. It's nice to see you two so enthusiastic about everything today,' said Mr Archer. 'Get changed and then you can get started.'

Ten minutes later, Ben and Steve were jogging round the school grounds wearing their PE kits and backpacks, watching the rest of their class play football.

'Why did you volunteer me for this? I'd rather play football,' Ben complained. 'I'd rather do maths come to that.'

'I'm not going to suffer alone,' Steve told him.

'Thanks.'

'You're welcome.'

With each step, Ben's bag bumped up and down on his back. And the strangest noises were coming from the bag. Like 'Ooof!' and 'Ouch!' and 'Yowwww!'

'Ben, I ache all over,' Whizziwig cried out. 'How much longer do we have to do this?'

'About another half an hour or so.'

'Why do I have to suffer with you?' Whizziwig grumbled.

Ben and Steve looked at each other and smiled maliciously. Whizziwig suffering with them was the silver lining to their big, dark cloud. They ran and Ran and RAN. Until not just a few drops of sweat but an entire river was running down Ben's forehead and he was sure his heart would explode out of his chest. Not soon enough, Mr Archer called a halt to the double PE lesson and sent them all back inside to get changed.

Steve and Ben collapsed, exhausted, on the benches in the changing rooms.

'Still want to join the SAS, Steve?' Mr Archer smiled.

'Not in this lifetime, sir, no,' Steve managed to gasp out.

Chapter Eight

Worth While

'I've never been so tired in my life.'

'My fingernails ache,' said Ben.

'My blood aches.'

'My hair aches.' Ben rubbed his head. It actually did feel as if his hair was aching!

'The air around me hurts.' Steve sighed. 'I won't be sorry to get to bed tonight.'

'You're sure you'll be OK? You won't go floating off in your sleep?'

'No.' Steve shook his head. 'I'll tie the bag to my feet and tie some books around my waist. That should keep me in the bed.'

'Never a dull moment.' Ben whistled.

'You said it!'

Ben and Steve walked on a bit further. Ben knew he had to pluck up the courage and say what he wanted to say now or he'd never say it at all.

'Steve, I'm sorry I had a go at you earlier,' Ben muttered. 'The truth is . . . I was a bit jealous.'

'Of what?' Steve was more than a little surprised.

'When Whizziwig offered you the chance to go flying with her, I think I went a bit Kermit the frog!'

'Green!' Steve laughed.

'I'm sorry too, Ben.' Whizziwig was floating alongside Ben and Steve now. 'But I can't take you. You're too heavy. That's why I never suggested it before.'

'Yes, I know. That's OK, Whizzy. You and Steve go flying. Just be careful, that's all.' Ben forced a smile. 'And have a good time – OK?'

Ben would've given anything to be able to fly with them. But there was no use dwelling on it, because it wasn't going to happen.

'Steve, how about having dinner at my house today?' Ben suggested. 'You'll be able to sit with your backpack on then. Mum and Dad are used to you acting like a weirdo, so they won't think anything of it.'

'Thanks!' Steve said with indignation.

When at last they reached Ben's home, Ben had to ring the doorbell. The front door opened and Mum disappeared in a blur into the living room. Ben was barely through the door before the smell hit him.

'Mum?' Ben ran straight into the living room. Mum was sitting on the sofa. 'Mum, what's that burning smell?'

'That was supposed to be tonight's dinner. It's the chicken in the oven. Only it caught fire, so I had to put it out using the fire extinguisher!' said Mum.

Ben frowned at Mum's tone of voice. She sounded very calm about it! Too calm.

'Mum, why're you sitting in here, staring at the wall?' asked Ben.

'The telly blew up when I tried to turn it on.'

Mum shrugged.

'What?' Ben walked over to the TV and pressed the ON/OFF switch. The telly came on at once and the picture was perfect.

'That just proves it. It's me!' said Mum. 'Well, I'm not going to move from this chair until your dad comes home. He can go and get Lizzie. I'm not risking it.'

'But, Mum, what're we going to eat?' Ben frowned. 'I invited Steve round for dinner.'

Mum leaned forward to look around Ben. 'Oh, hi, Steve. You're welcome to stay for dinner, but I'm not cooking. I'll order a pizza to be delivered. OK?'

'Great! Thanks, Mrs Sinclair!' Steve grinned.

'Thanks, Mum.'

Dad didn't arrive home until they'd already eaten their pizzas. Ben and Steve were out in the garden when they heard his voice.

'Hello, darling. Why the long face?' asked Dad.

'Oh, Daniel!' Mum threw herself into Dad's arms. 'I've had such a miserable day. I locked myself out of the house. I fell in a duck pond. I tried to go and pick up Lizzie and the car wouldn't start. And then when I called someone out to look at it, it worked first time. Then the chicken in the oven blew up and the telly decided to do the same out of sympathy!'

'Never mind, dear.' Dad smiled and gave Mum a big kiss. 'I've got a surprise for you. This will cheer you up. To make up for not being able to take the day off, I've arranged for Aunt Dottie to take the kids this Saturday. Then I'll treat you to the cinema or the theatre, followed by a slap-up meal. How does that sound?'

'Wonderful.' Mum's face lit up like a lighthouse. 'Oh, Daniel!'

And Mum and Dad started kissing again.

Ben, Whizziwig and Steve were watching through the kitchen window. It was beginning to get a bit dark outside, but even if it'd been broad daylight, Ben's mum and dad wouldn't have noticed them. They were too busy kissing!

'Your mum and dad are really into all that lovey-dovey stuff, aren't they?' said Steve.

'I know,' Ben said glumly. 'I've begged them to stop. If they knew how embarrassing it is to watch two old people like them kissing and cuddling all the time, I'm sure they wouldn't do it!'

'I think it's sweet!' Whizziwig sighed.

Ben and Steve just looked at her.

'You two had better get cracking if you're going to go flying before it gets too dark,' Ben pointed out.

Ben tied a piece of string around Whizziwig's wrist and then around Steve's wrist. Ben held on to the dangling end just to be on the safe side. He'd let go once Steve had got the hang of not having his feet on the ground.

Whizziwig began to rise into the air. Steve followed her up and up.

'Whoo-oooaaa!' Steve put out his arms to steady himself. Then he grinned. 'This is great!'

Ben chewed his bottom lip, then immediately stopped. If Steve saw him do that, he'd know that Ben was upset. It just wasn't fair. Steve was about a metre off the ground now.

'Are you OK? Shall I let go of the string?' Ben asked.

Steve looked down at Ben and his smile faded. 'I wish you could come with us.'

Whizziwig's eyes sparkled. The wish was granted. Ben began to rise into the air.

'Wow! Thanks, Steve.' Ben beamed at him.

'I wish I'd thought of wishing that before!' Steve smiled back.

Ben tied the dangling bit of string around his own wrist and the three friends rose higher and higher into the air.

'Isn't this great?' Whizziwig called out.

Great wasn't the word for it. It was wonderful! Brilliant! *Cool!*

'Let's loop the loop,' Ben suggested.

'Let's what?' asked Whizziwig.

'Follow me.' Ben rose up to take the lead until they were high enough, then he dived down and flew back up again, doing a complete somersault.

'Yahoo!' Ben shouted.

'I don't know what that means,' said Whizziwig, 'but it's just how I feel! Let's do it again.'

So they looped the loop again, all yelling 'YAHOO!' – and meaning every letter of it!

'D'you know something?' Steve said as they flew above the trees. 'Today hasn't been so bad after all!'

And then there was the time that . . .

Chapter Nine

Dinner at Aunt Dottie's

'**B**en, are you sure your Aunt Dorothy won't mind me coming round for dinner?'

Ben smiled at his best friend. 'We call her Dottie for short. And stop worrying. Aunt Dottie always cooks enough to feed an army.'

Ben rang the doorbell, adding under his

breath, 'Besides, why should I suffer alone?'

'What was that?' Steve's ears were better than Ben had thought.

'I hope I won't be stuck in your bag all afternoon,' Whizziwig grumbled. 'I see more of your smelly bag than any other place on Earth.'

Before Ben could say a word, the front door opened. And there Aunt Dottie stood, with a slice of bread balanced on her head. Ben risked a quick glance at Steve, hoping that he hadn't noticed. Though from the stunned look on Steve's face, Ben was wasting his time hoping any such thing!

'Hi, Aunt Dottie. How are you?' Ben sighed. He was used to Aunt Dottie's strange behaviour, but he could see why it might come as a shock to other people who didn't know her. As Dad always said, 'Dottie by name and Dottie by nature!'

'Hello, Ben. I'm fine.' Aunt Dottie smiled. 'Did you brush your teeth today?'

'Yes,' Ben replied, surprised.

'Then you can give me a kiss!' said Aunt Dottie, offering her cheek. She looked at Steve with suspicion. 'Are you selling something? 'Cause if you are, I'll take two.'

'No, I'm . . . I'm Steve. Ben's my best friend,' Steve stammered.

'Did you brush your teeth today?'

'Yes,' squeaked Steve.

'Then you can give me a kiss.' Aunt Dottie smiled, offering her cheek.

'Aunt Dottie, why have you got a slice of bread on your head?' Ben had to know.

'It's to remind me to buy a loaf of bread tomorrow afternoon.'

'Why don't you just write it down?' Ben asked. That was what a normal person would do, he couldn't help thinking.

'But then I'd forget where I'd left the note – silly!' said Aunt Dottie, squeezing his cheek. She looked up and down the road. 'Come in! Come in! You never know how many invisible people may be listening!'

Ben and Steve went into the house. Ben had to bite his lip to stop himself from laughing at the expression on Steve's face. Steve looked like he wasn't sure what he was letting himself in for.

'I've got a surprise for both of you,' said Aunt Dottie, ushering them into the living room. 'Look what I bought myself!'

'A piano!' exclaimed Ben.

'That's right.' Aunt Dottie walked across the room to stroke it lovingly. 'Isn't it beautiful?'

'Can I have a go?' Ben asked.

'After me. Sit! Sit! You're in for a treat. I'm going to play it for you.'

Ben and Steve sat down on the sofa, which had been moved round to face the piano rather than the telly. Aunt Dottie ran her fingers over the closed lid before she carefully lifted it.

'Ready?' she asked, her fingers poised on the keys.

Steve and Ben nodded. Aunt Dottie began. And what a racket! She slammed her hands on to the keys and plonked them up and down the octaves, making a dreadful noise. But worse was to come! She started singing – if it could be called singing, which Ben sincerely thought it couldn't. The din was so horrible that Aunt Dottie's cat, who had been asleep under the radiator, sprang up and raced from the room in fright.

Aunt Dottie stopped playing and singing to frown. 'What's the matter with Sir Galahad?'

'Sir Galahad?' Steve asked.

'The cat,' Ben explained.

'Maybe he's a music lover!' Steve said under his breath.

Ben elbowed him in the ribs.

'Now then, where was I?' Aunt Dottie raised her hands to punish the piano keys, and Ben and Steve's eardrums, once again.

'Aunt Dottie!' Ben sprang out of his chair. 'Shall I go and check on the dinner?'

'NO! I mean, I'll do it.' Steve leapt out of his chair as well. 'Just point me towards the kitchen.'

'There's no need for either of you to move a muscle.' Aunt Dottie motioned for them to sit down. 'The kidney and banana casserole is already in the oven. And I've made a lovely lettuce and treacle salad to go with it.'

And with that, Aunt Dottie started playing the piano again. Ben sank down into his chair, trying to think of some way to get out of the room and also get out of eating his dinner.

'Ben, she hasn't really made all that stuff, has she?' Steve whispered. 'That was a joke – right?'

Slowly, Ben shook his head.

'You said your aunt was a wonderful cook.'

'She is – if you don't have any taste-buds.'

Steve glared at Ben. 'Thanks a bunch.'

'Sorry.' Ben shrugged. 'I needed moral support.'

Inside Ben's bag, Whizziwig was spinning round and round, trying to bury herself under Ben's books and smelly PE socks to get away from Aunt Dottie's awful racket. She wasn't having much luck!

'I'm sorry, Ben, but I can't take any more!' said Whizziwig, floating out of Ben's bag behind Aunt Dottie's back. 'Bye!'

'Whizziwig, you can't . . .'

Ignoring him, Whizziwig floated across the carpet and out of the door.

'She's got the right idea,' Steve fumed. 'I'll never let you forget this, Ben. Never.'

Ben slumped back in his chair. Now he was in trouble with both Whizziwig and Steve. And from what Aunt Dottie had just said, his stomach was in trouble too. What next?

Chapter Ten

The Switch

Ben and Steve were walking to school – but that was all they were doing. Ben was absolutely furious. And he certainly wasn't going to be the first one to speak.

'Oh, for goodness' sake. I said I was sorry.' Steve sighed. 'How many times d'you want me to say it? I'm sorry! I'm sorry! Besides, I think

I got away with it.'

'Got away with it!' Ben rounded on Steve. 'Aunt Dottie knew full well that you didn't like her cooking.'

'How?'

'Throwing up all over her cat was a subtle clue!'

Steve looked embarrassed. 'Well, I tried to get to the bathroom again, but I didn't see Sir Galahad lying in the doorway.'

'Hang on – what d'you mean *again*?' Ben asked. 'You were sick more than once?'

Steve nodded.

'I hope you made it to the bathroom the first time then.'

Steve shook his head.

Ben closed his eyes. 'How far *did* you get?'

'The hall. I was sick in your aunt's yucca plant.'

Whizziwig wrinkled up her nose. 'Yeuch!'

'No, yucca!' Steve grinned.

'Thanks a lot for showing me up.' Ben stormed off ahead. 'Aunt Dottie will never let me hear the end of it. You shouldn't have wolfed down your food so fast. Then it wouldn't have made you sick.'

Steve slowed down so he wouldn't have to listen to Ben rant at him. Ben marched on ahead, not realizing that Steve was no longer walking beside him.

'If you'd chewed it more slowly, it would've stayed down,' Ben continued.

'Nag! Whinge! Moan! Gripe! Complain!' Steve muttered to Whizziwig, who was floating between them.

'He's not too happy with you, is he?' Whizziwig wagged a finger at Steve.

'It wasn't my fault. Ben should've warned me about his aunt's cooking. Then I could've prepared my stomach.'

'How?'

'By taping my lips together!' Steve replied.

Only when Ben was several metres ahead did he realize that he was talking to himself. He turned back, an irate look on his face. 'Come on, Steve. We're going to be late for school at this rate.'

'For goodness' sake, put a sock in it!' Steve called back, annoyed. 'I wish you came with an ON/OFF switch! I really do!'

'Maybe if I'm lucky, Aunt Dottie hasn't noticed her . . .' Ben suddenly stopped talking in mid-sentence. And he stood absolutely still, like a statue.

'Look, I've said I'm sorry. How many more times?' Steve walked up to Ben. 'Ben? Ben, what's the . . .' Steve noticed the strange switch in the middle of Ben's forehead. 'What on earth is that? Ben? Ben!' Steve shook Ben's arm, but it just flopped at Ben's side.

And only then did Steve realize what had happened.

'Whizziwig!' Steve stared. 'You didn't!'

'I did.'

Steve pressed the switch on Ben's forehead.

'. . . yucca plant yet.' Ben finished his earlier sentence. 'If I can get round there and clean it up before she notices, then she might let both of us in her house again.' Ben looked from Steve to Whizziwig and back again. 'Why are you two giving me funny looks?'

'D'you want to tell him or shall I?' asked Whizziwig.

'Tell me what?'

Steve pointed, his expression, his whole body apologetic. 'You've got an ON/OFF switch in the middle of your forehead.'

'I've got a what?' Ben clapped his hand to his

forehead. Unfortunately, he clapped just a little too hard and switched himself off again.

Steve moved Ben's hand out of the way and switched him back on.

Ben blinked rapidly. He knew what must've happened. He'd switched himself 'off'. His eyes shooting out sparks, Ben turned to Whizziwig. 'Tell me you didn't.'

'Sorry! But I did!' Whizziwig shrugged.

Chapter Eleven

A Bad Mood
and a Shock

'Great! Just great! Look at my forehead.'
Ben raged.

'Sorry. I didn't mean for Whizziwig to
actually do it.'

'Lucky for me, I'm very efficient.' Whizziwig
was obviously very proud of herself.

Ben, Steve and Whizziwig were in the boys' toilets at school and it was the first time Ben had had a chance to see the result of Steve's wish.

'How am I meant to walk around all day with this thing on my head?' Ben carried on. 'I look like a baby unicorn!'

Steve was saved from answering by the school buzzer.

'We'd better go. We don't want to be late for registration,' said Steve.

Ben walked along the corridor with his hand cupped over his forehead. He didn't want to risk switching himself off again, nor did he want anyone else to see the switch. Something told him that today wasn't going to be the easiest school day he'd ever had. Ben and Steve reached the classroom just as Mr Archer was coming along the corridor. And Mr Archer had a face like thunder. They ducked into the classroom before their teacher could reach them.

'Steve, I've got to do something about this switch. I can't keep my hand over it all the time. My arm is getting tired.'

'Let's go to the school nurse after the lesson.

Maybe she can put a plaster on it,' Steve suggested.

'Good idea,' Ben agreed.

'All right, class. I don't want any nonsense this morning. Do I make myself clear?' said Mr Archer.

'Yes, Mr Archer,' a few people in the class replied feebly.

'I said, "Is that clear?"' Mr Archer boomed.

'Yes, Mr Archer,' everyone shouted.

'That's better,' Mr Archer snapped.

'Wow! He's in a good mood this morning,' Steve whispered

'There's a lot of it about,' Ben said sourly.

'Everyone take out your *History Today* class books and turn to page fifty-seven.' Mr Archer glared around the classroom.

As he dug into his bag for his book, Ben wondered what was the matter with his teacher. Mr Archer wasn't usually so grouchy.

'Ben, what's that thing on your face?'

At the sound of his teacher's voice, Ben looked up from his bag. 'What thing, sir?'

'That thing.' Mr Archer pressed the switch on Ben's forehead. 'Well? What is it?'

Ben didn't answer. He was 'off'!

'Ben, I'm talking to you.' Mr Archer frowned.

Steve quickly pressed Ben's switch, saying, 'It's for a science project, Mr Archer.'

Ben was confused. 'What's for a science project?'

'We're not having science now.' Mr Archer's frown deepened. 'So you can just take it off.'

Mr Archer tugged at the switch.

'OOH! OUCH! YOW!' Ben cried out.

And suddenly he was silent. Mr Archer had switched him 'off' again!

'It won't come off, sir. We've tried.' Steve pressed Ben's switch. 'The glue we used to put it on was stronger than we thought.'

'Ben, go and see the school nurse during break-time. I don't want that thing on your face disrupting our lessons,' snapped Mr Archer.

'No, sir,' Ben replied. Changing it to, 'Yes, sir,' at the look on Mr Archer's face.

Hopefully once he had a plaster on his forehead covering up the ridiculous switch, he'd be safe from everyone he met pressing it to see what it was. Just as long as nothing else . . .

The classroom door opened. Miss Jute

walked in. Ben's jaw hit his table when he saw who was behind her. It was Aunt Dottie.

'Auntie! What're you doing here?' Ben asked, aghast.

'I'm a classroom helper. I volunteered.' Aunt Dottie cupped one hand over her mouth and whispered in a voice that rang out throughout the classroom, 'Ben, what's that on your forehead?'

Ben couldn't answer. A classroom helper? His aunt was a classroom helper. Oh, no! What next?

'Oh, Miss Jute . . . I . . . er . . . Good morning, Miss Jute.' Mr Archer flushed red and stammered.

'Good morning, class,' Miss Jute said, completely ignoring Mr Archer. 'This is Mrs Allen. She'll be your classroom helper for the day.'

'Aunt Dottie, you can't,' Ben pleaded.

'Yes, I can. Watch me.' Aunt Dottie smiled.

'Now, if you'll excuse me,' said Miss Jute. And with that she headed for the door. Mr Archer was two steps behind her.

'Er, Miss Jute, just a moment,' said Mr Archer.

He followed her out of the classroom, closing the door behind him. Aunt Dottie stood at the front of the class, looking around uncertainly. But that lasted only a moment.

'Hi, everyone. I'm Dottie!'

Practically everyone in the class started to titter. Ben felt his face begin to burn.

'I'm Ben's great-aunt. He's cute, isn't he?'

'Auntie!' Ben looked around to find that all eyes were upon him. There'd been a lot of that recently! He might've guessed that this would happen. Aunt Dottie had been in his classroom for all of ten seconds and she was already showing him up.

'Ben, you are cute!' Aunt Dottie argued. 'In fact, when you were a baby, I remember saying to your mum and dad that they could put a baby bonnet round your bottom instead of your face and everyone would still think you were the cutest!'

The whole class erupted with laughter. Even Steve was laughing like a drain. Ben glared at him and Steve bit his lip to try and stop. Ben glared around the class and then at his aunt. Charlotte was laughing too. She was going to have great fun teasing him mercilessly about this one. He'd never be able to live it down. Never, ever!

Thanks, Aunt Dottie, he fumed. Thanks a lot!

Chapter Twelve

Reasons

'Miss Jute, a moment please,' Mr Archer said very formally outside his classroom. He had to be formal because Mrs Jenkins, another teacher, was walking past. But the moment that Mrs Jenkins was out of earshot, his tone altered.

'Judy, what's the matter?'

'Nothing, Leonard,' Miss Jute replied frostily.

Mr Archer opened his mouth to argue, but just at that moment a girl came charging round the corner towards them.

'Walk, Saffron! Don't run.' Mr Archer glared.

'But I'm late, sir,' Saffron puffed.

'Then walk fast, but don't run,' Mr Archer ordered.

Saffron walked past Mr Archer and Miss Jute at a brisk pace until she turned the corner, when she started running again – just as Mr Archer had known she would.

'Judy, what did I do? Why won't you talk to me?' Mr Archer lowered his voice.

'You really don't know, do you?'

Mr Archer shook his head.

Miss Jute glared at him. 'When we first started going out together, I thought you were so . . . so romantic.'

'I am.' Mr Archer's cheeks glowed red like traffic lights.

'You wouldn't know romance if it bit you on both ankles. I'm disappointed in you, Leonard. Very disappointed. Excuse me.' And with that Miss Jute swept past Mr Archer, her nose almost bumping off the ceiling.

Behind him, Mr Archer could hear his class roaring with laughter. He walked back into his classroom. Instant silence.

'That's better. And let's just keep it that way,' he snapped.

'What would you like me to do, Mr Archer. I read, I write, I sing, I play the piano, I play hopscotch. Just put me to good use.' Aunt Dottie smiled.

'You play the piano?'

'That's right. Ben and Steve will tell you. I was playing for them only last night.'

'Well, in that case,' began Mr Archer, 'I wonder if I might ask you for a favour. Could you play the piano and sing for us in our assembly this afternoon?'

'Oh, no!' the hushed words tumbled out of Ben's mouth.

'It's just that Mr Clancy, who usually plays the piano, is off sick this week,' Mr Archer continued.

'She can't. You can't, can you, Aunt Dottie? You've lost your voice,' Ben tried.

'No, I haven't. Here it is! La-la-la-la-la-la-la-la!'

'But you can't play the piano because . . .

because you trapped your fingers in the fridge door last night and now they're really hurting.'

'No, they're not. They're fine. See!' Aunt Dottie linked her fingers together and then stretched them out, making the bones crack. Mr Archer winced. 'Mr Archer, I'd love to do it. Just tell me what, where and when.'

'But, Aunt Dottie –'

Mr Archer had had enough. 'Ben, d'you mind? Besides, this is none of your business.'

'But, sir –'

'I said that's enough.'

And Ben knew better than to keep arguing. He listened, dismayed, as Mr Archer directed Aunt Dottie to the hall so that she could practise on the piano there.

'Ben,' Steve said urgently.

'I know! I know!' Ben hissed back. It was bad enough when Aunt Dottie made a fool of him, but he couldn't sit back and watch her make a fool of herself – he just couldn't. What was he going to do?

Chapter Thirteen

From Bad
To Worse

At break-time, Steve and Ben went to see Mrs Torin, the school nurse. Ben knocked on the door and she opened it, a cup of tea in her hand.

'Mrs Torin, could you do something about this swi – thing on my head?' Ben asked.

'It . . . it looks like a switch!' Mrs Torin frowned.

'No. It's just a funny spot,' Ben said.

'Hhmm! It's the funniest spot I've ever seen. Well, come in then. I'll see what I can do.'

Both Steve and Ben tried to walk inside the room.

'Steve, where d'you think you're going?' asked Mrs Torin. 'You can wait for Ben outside.' She firmly shut the door in his face and took Ben over towards the light, reaching out a hand to touch the switch.

'Oh, please don't touch it. It's . . . it's very sore,' Ben said quickly.

'OK. I'll put a plaster on it,' said Mrs Torin.

Ben watched as she tore off a strip of pink plaster. 'Could you be very careful not to touch it please?'

With great care, Mrs Torin applied the plaster, pressing down hard on either side to get it to stick. Ben turned to look at himself in the wall mirror.

'The plaster is really noticeable.' Ben frowned. 'It's almost as bad as the switch . . . I mean, spot. Don't you have any brown plasters?'

Mrs Torin shook her head. 'No. Sorry!'

'I guess it'll have to do.' Ben sighed.

One side of the plaster was already beginning to peel off.

'Here. Let me,' said Mrs Torin.

Before Ben could stop her, she pressed the plaster back on to Ben's forehead. Unfortunately, she pressed the switch at the same time. Ben was 'off'!

'There you go.' Mrs Torin smiled.

Ben didn't reply. He stood still, staring at Mrs Torin.

'Ben, are you all right?'

Ben didn't answer.

'Ben?' Mrs Torin put a worried hand on Ben's shoulder and gave him a shake. Ben keeled over backwards like a felled tree.

The door flew open.

'What was that crash?' Steve stood in the doorway, staring down at Ben. 'Not again!'

'Steve, quick! Run to the staff room and tell them to phone for an ambulance. Ben's had an allergic reaction to the plaster I put on his forehead.'

Steve stared at Ben, who was lying on the floor, staring up at the ceiling.

'Steve, move!' Mrs Torin urged.

'No, I . . . I . . . You don't understand.'

'Look! Stay with him. I'll do it.' Mrs Torin raced down the corridor.

Steve didn't waste a moment. He ran into the room and ripped the plaster off Ben's forehead. Then he pressed the switch. Puzzled, Ben sat up.

'What am I doing on the. . .' Ben's hand flew to the back of his head. 'Ow! That hurts.' His hand moved to his sore forehead. 'Ouch! So does this!'

'Quick! Stand up! Come on.'

Ben scrambled to his feet. 'What's the matter?'

Steve explained as he and Ben raced down the corridor. They managed to catch up with Mrs Torin about five metres away from the staff room.

'Mrs Torin, it's OK – see? Ben's fine,' Steve called out.

Mrs Torin stared. 'Ben? You were out cold. You . . .'

'No, I'm fine. Honest.'

'We've got to go out, miss, or we'll miss our break-time,' Steve said quickly.

'Bye.'

And Mrs Torin could only watch bemused as Ben and Steve dashed off.

Well, at least Ben could put a plaster over his switch, so that was one weight off his mind, but something else a lot more pressing had taken its place. Aunt Dottie! He had to come up with a way – and fast – to stop her singing.

'Whizziwig, about Aunt Dottie . . .' Ben removed his bag from his shoulder and opened it 'I don't suppose –'

'Don't even think about it!' Whizziwig sniffed. 'I didn't come all the way to this planet to stop you getting embarrassed.'

'I was only asking!' Ben told her. 'There's no need to bite my head clean off my neck!'

Steve and Ben walked along the corridor, deep in thought.

'We've got about two minutes left of our break-time – if we're lucky,' Steve grumbled as they passed their classroom.

Ben happened to glance in, then he stopped short. 'Look! Who's that in our classroom? That's Trump, isn't it?'

Ben opened the door. Trump turned around. He had GUILTY written all over his face.

'What're you doing in here, Trump? This is

our classroom, not yours.' Steve frowned.

'I was looking for something.'

'Oh, yeah?' Ben raised his eyebrows.

'Yeah! And I've found it now, so I'm off.'

Ben and Steve stepped aside as Trump pushed past them and sauntered down the corridor. They exchanged a look before following him out of the room. Why had he been in their classroom? Just what had he been up to? At that moment the buzzer sounded.

'So much for our break-time,' said Ben, and sighed.

They sat down at their table. For once they were going to be the first ones rather than the last to arrive back from break. But the mood Mr Archer was in, he'd still probably find a reason to have a go at them.

Chapter Fourteen

Inspiring

Mr Archer was the last one to enter the classroom and, from the thunderous expression on his face, he hadn't mellowed out one iota.

'I didn't want any nonsense this morning and I don't want any now either,' Mr Archer snapped.

'Good grief!' whispered Steve. 'I wish he'd chill out a bit.'

Mr Archer visibly shivered and picked up his jacket, which was hanging over the back of his chair. He put it on and pulled it tightly around himself.

'Charlotte, could you shut the windows please? It's freezing in here.'

Charlotte gasped. 'But, sir, it's not. It's baking. It's fifty million degrees in here.'

Mr Archer pointed at the two open windows. 'Charlotte, if you don't mind.' And his tone made it very clear that even if she did mind, he wanted the windows closed. Everyone groaned. Charlotte stood up and did as she was told. A few brave ones in the class started to fan themselves to make the point. Ben and Steve bent under their table. Whizziwig grinned up at them from Ben's bag.

'Whizziwig, that's not what Steve meant,' Ben hissed.

'I just wanted Mr Archer to stop snapping and being so miserable. I didn't want him to be chilly,' Steve explained.

'That's not what you said,' Whizziwig pointed out.

'That's what I meant,' Steve whispered crossly.

'Well, it's too late now,' Whizziwig said.

'But with the windows shut, this room will turn into a sauna,' Ben protested.

Mr Archer's head appeared under the table. Ben only just had time to shut his bag.

'Is this a private under-the-table conversation or can anyone join in?' drawled Mr Archer.

Immediately, Ben and Steve tried to sit up. They both banged their heads on the underside of the table. Mr Archer came out from under the table first, followed by Ben and Steve, who were rubbing the backs of their heads.

'Now, if you could all take out your *Poetry Today* books and turn to page twelve,' said Mr Archer.

'This would be a good time to use the ON/OFF switch!' Ben whispered.

Steve could only nod his agreement.

'Charlotte, could you read please?' Mr Archer pulled his jacket tightly around his chest as he spoke.

Charlotte stood up. 'Fear no more the heat o' the sun. Nor the furious winter's rages. Thou thy worldly task hast done. Home art gone and ta'en thy wages.'

'Thank you, Charlotte.' Mr Archer sighed. 'Isn't that beautiful language?'

Mr Archer didn't seem to notice the few in the class who shook their heads!

'Oh, yes, sir,' Charlotte enthused. 'I wish we all spoke like that! It's so romantic. So inspiring!'

Ben and Steve stared in horror at each other. Ben could only pray that Whizziwig had shut down to recharge her primary energy.

'Indeed, Charlotte! Verily, thou speak the truth,' said Mr Archer.

'I thank thee, sir,' Charlotte replied.

Ben ducked under the table. 'Gadzooks, Whizziwig! What hast thou done, thou meddlesome hover ball?'

'Only what Charlotte wished for.' Whizziwig grinned. 'Really, there's no stopping me today!'

That's the trouble, Ben thought.

Chapter Fifteen

Overheard

Surprisingly enough, the rest of the lesson went really well. Ben could only suppose that somehow the way they were all speaking had cheered Mr Archer up. By the time the buzzer sounded, their teacher almost had a smile on his face. Almost!

While Mr Archer and the others trooped out

of the room, Ben gathered up his things, wondering what his mum and dad were going to make of the strange way he was speaking. They'd probably think it was wonderful too! He noticed that Charlotte was busy searching in her bag for something that was obviously being very elusive.

'Mistress Charlotte, what misfortune furrows thy brow?' Ben asked.

''Tis indeed strange, but this very morning did I purchase some vanilla bonbons and now I find them as absent as Mr Archer's sense of humour.'

Steve and Ben looked at each other. They were thinking the same thing.

'Absent? For truth?' asked Steve.

'Missing,' Charlotte confirmed.

'As if by vanilla-scented sticky fingers?' asked Steve.

'Quite so.' Charlotte nodded.

'I would wager we know the villain,' Ben said to Steve.

Nodding to each other, they stood up and left the classroom. Trump wasn't going to get away with it! Ben and Steve made their way out into the school grounds. As they looked around, their expressions grim, they saw Trump coming round a corner from the outside boys' toilets. He held a bag of sweets in his hands and, as they watched, popped one into his mouth.

'Aha! I do spy him.' Ben pointed.

'Let's have at him,' said Steve.

They ran over to Trump. The only thing Ben had in his mind was rescuing Charlotte's sweets.

'Are not those the confections of the lady who even now bewails their loss?' asked Steve.

'Indeed, I do believe they are the very same,' Ben said with disgust. 'And this dog's bum did help himself to them. You cur! You knave! You saucy fellow!'

'You what?' said Trump.

'Those are Charlotte's bonbons, are they not?' Ben said sternly.

'It would appear so. They are most vanilla in hue.' Steve prodded Trump in the shoulder. 'You, sir, are a gorbellied rogue!'

'You what?' said Trump.

'Verily, I shall relieve thee of them at once.' Ben snatched back the bag of bonbons.

'And be grateful we don't render upon thee the duffing thou so richly deserve.' Steve told him.

And with that, Ben and Steve marched off with a musketeer-ish swagger.

'You what?' Trump called after them, totally baffled.

Ben was fed up. Lunch-time was ticking away and he still hadn't found Charlotte to give her back her bonbons. Just as he and Steve were about to pass the assembly hall, they heard a horrible noise – like a cat in agony. Ben opened the door. Aunt Dottie was singing. Wincing, Ben closed the door again. He didn't see Aunt Dottie glance up and catch sight of him, just at that moment.

Ben walked away from the assembly hall even more dejected than before.

He and Steve were turning the corner to go to the canteen for their lunch when Ben suddenly leaned back against the wall.

'Woe is me. I am undone!' he wailed.

Steve glanced down at his friend's trousers. 'No. Thy flies are intact!'

'Not my flies, dolt! My reputation. My good name. My character.'

'Prithee, what're you on about?' Steve frowned.

'You grasp not my meaning?'

Steve shook his head.

'Then I will say it plain. If a crow with laryngitis is a singer, then my aunt is a singer. If a shovel dragged across a gravel floor makes a singer, then my aunt is indeed a singer. She cannot sing, my friend. I love my auntie dear, but her singing doth suck!'

'So what will you do?' asked Steve.

Ben shrugged. 'There is nothing I can do. Aunt Dottie has been asked to sing and sing she will.'

'Come.' Steve put his arm around Ben's shoulder. 'We cannot find Charlotte and lunchtime will soon be over. Let us dine on the swill they call school dinners.'

'That's right! Cheer me up!'

Ben and Steve carried on walking down the corridor. But just around the corner from them stood Aunt Dottie. And she'd heard every word.

Chapter Sixteen

The Proposal

'I don't want to go to lunch with you,' Whizziwig protested from inside Ben's bag. 'I want to recharge my primary energy and I don't want to be bumped about on your back while I do it.'

'I hear thee!' Ben told her. 'Keep thy fur on!'

Ben and Steve headed back to their

classroom. Ben put his bag, with Whizziwig in it, under his table.

'I'll see thee anon, Whizziwig. After my repast,' said Ben.

'Can you say that in English please?' asked Whizziwig.

'I'll see thee later, after lunch,' said Ben, fighting to get the modern words out.

'Oh, OK!' Whizziwig ducked down under Ben's table and closed her eyes.

Ben and Steve left the room. Seconds later the classroom door opened again. Annoyed, Whizziwig opened her eyes.

How am I meant to recharge my primary energy with Ben and Steve constantly interrupting me? Whizziwig thought crossly. She floated out from beneath the table, ready to give them a piece of her mind. Only it wasn't Ben and Steve – it was Aunt Dottie. Whizziwig ducked straight back down under the table – and only just in time. Aunt Dottie flopped into Mr Archer's chair to get her handbag out of his bottom drawer.

'Are my piano playing and singing really that bad?' Aunt Dottie asked herself. 'I guess they must be if Ben says so. How am I going to get out of this? I'll just have to tell Mr Archer . . . But I said I'd do it. I'm sorry now I opened my mouth. I wish I could play the piano properly, so Ben won't be ashamed of me.'

Whizziwig's eyes sparkled. The wish was granted.

'And I thought my singing was good.' Aunt Dottie sighed. 'Not exactly Whitney Houston – but close!'

Aunt Dottie got up and headed for the staff room. Try as she might, she just couldn't figure out a way to tell Mr Archer that she wouldn't be able to play or sing any more. She slunk into the staff room and chose the remotest corner so that she could sit by herself and think.

Mr Archer was in the staff room, pretending to read a newspaper. When Miss Jute went to make herself a cup of tea, he sprang up and followed her.

'Er, Judy,' Mr Archer spoke softly while looking around. 'Judy, I would crave a moment of thy time.'

'Yes, Leonard.' Miss Jute's voice dripped with frost.

'The gentle sun of thy smile has turned to

frosty winter and I must know the reason for it!' said Mr Archer.

Miss Jute glared at him. 'If by that you mean why am I mad at you, then I'll tell you. On our last date, I had my hair done especially and I wore a brand-new dress that cost me an arm and both legs – and you didn't notice. I spent all day trying to look nice and you didn't say a word.'

'Forgive me, Judy. Weighty matters preyed upon my mind that day.'

'Like what?' Miss Jute folded her arms across her chest.

Embarrassed, Mr Archer looked around. 'This is no place for a discussion of tender matters. Can't we discuss this away from prying eyes and flapping ears?'

'Here and now are just fine,' Miss Jute stated. 'I want to know what you had on your mind, because it certainly wasn't me.'

'But it was. I mean, you were. Judy! Thy very name is the tinkling of tiny bells. Thy temperament is rare, like a tree filled with shells! There's something I must tell thee, something thou should know. Thy eyes are the sun's golden rise and the moon's silver glow. Thy hair smells of cinnamon and freshly baked bread!'

Miss Jute patted her hair, unsure about the last description.

'Thy lips are like rubies rare or sweet cherries red!' Mr Archer went down on one knee. He didn't seem to notice that he had the attention of the entire staff room. 'Judy, won't thou answer me before I count to ten. Darling, marry me and I shall be the happiest of men!'

'Oh, Leonard!' There were tears in Miss Jute's eyes. 'How could I have thought you were unromantic. Of course I'll marry you.'

Mr Archer got to his feet and he and Miss Jute hugged each other right then and there. The male teachers in the staff room sighed at the romance of it all, while the female teachers looked at each other and mimed being violently sick.

Chapter Seventeen

For the Best

Mr Archer practically danced into the classroom, a face-splitting grin all over his face.

'Good afternoon, class. Isn't it a beautiful day – even if the weather doth freeze the very marrow in my bones? Charlotte, close yonder window, I entreat thee.'

Reluctantly, Charlotte did as she was told.

'Now, I hope thou art all ready for this afternoon's assembly. I believe we are in for a treat!' said Mr Archer.

'Methinks our teacher has lost his marbles!' said Ben sourly. 'Methinks Mr Archer is going to wish he'd come to school with earplugs.'

'Line up, everyone,' Mr Archer said cheerily.

Ben grabbed his bag and stood in line next to Steve, still trying desperately to come up with a way of saving himself and his aunt from school-wide embarrassment and humiliation.

All too soon, everyone from the junior school trooped into the assembly hall. Ben looked up at his aunt on the stage. He was surprised to see she looked nervous. Very nervous. At last everyone had settled down and all eyes were on Aunt Dottie. She ran her fingers over the piano lid, before raising it up. Ben pulled at one side of the plaster on his forehead. His finger was just about to press down on his switch when Steve grabbed his hand.

'Oh no, thou dost not! If we needst suffer, then thou must suffer also!' Steve told him.

Ben gave up. He hid his face behind his hands. Steve did the same. He'd just have to grit his teeth and bear it. Aunt Dottie ran her fingers up and down the scales. Then she began to play. And she was brilliant! Amazing! Stunning! Ben's hands fell to his sides. His jaw dropped open. And his wasn't the only one. Ben lifted his bag on to his lap.

'Whizzy, do I spy thy hand in this?'

'Your aunt wished that she could play properly so that she wouldn't embarrass you,' Whizziwig whispered.

'She said that?' Ben asked, surprised.

'She did.'

Ben looked up at his aunt. 'She is indeed brilliant – and I do not merely speak of her piano playing.'

Mr Archer scowled in Ben's direction. 'Hush up!'

Ben bit his lip and looked back at his aunt. She chose that moment to look around, and all she could see were enthralled expressions on the faces of her audience. The worried look on her face vanished, to be replaced by a relieved smile.

'Ben, I think I should warn you . . .' Whizziwig began.

Too late! Aunt Dottie began to sing. And she was *dreadful*. Just as bad, if not worse than before.

'. . . your aunt never wished anything about her singing!' Whizziwig finished her sentence.

Ben looked around. Others in the hall were wincing and flinching at Aunt Dottie's 'singing', but Ben discovered that he didn't mind one bit.

'What's the problem?' Ben smiled. 'To my ears she is the very spit of Scary Spice!'

'Verily, the scary part is right,' Steve agreed.

'Steve, thy ears have more wax in them than Madame Tussaud's,' Ben told his friend.

'D'you know? Your aunt sings a bit like me,' Whizziwig said.

''Twas my very point,' Steve muttered.

'Hardly! Besides, if my aunt loves to sing, how can we do otherwise than love it also?'

'Like this, mate!' grumbled Steve.

Ben sat back in his chair to enjoy his aunt's singing, even though those around him were obviously suffering. Aunt Dottie looked at him and winked before continuing. Ben smiled back. There was no doubt about it. Aunt Dottie was terrific!

And what about the time when . . .

Chapter Eighteen

Put Yourself In My Place

For a Friday afternoon, the classroom was unusually quiet. Everyone was busy doing a mid-term test. Mr Archer sat at his table, reading a book called *Weddings! What Every Groom Should Know*. Suddenly he lowered his book, a suspicious look on his face. His eyes narrowed, as if in the hope of catching someone doing something they shouldn't be doing.

Underneath Ben's table, Whizziwig was reading a science fiction comic in which the baddies were hunting an alien who looked a bit like her.

'Urgghhh! Where do humans get their ideas from?' Whizziwig muttered, unimpressed.

Ben's head suddenly appeared under the table. 'Shush!' Ben returned to his test.

'Sir?'

Ben turned to find Emma waving her hand in the air, trying to attract Mr Archer's attention. He went hot all over. She hadn't seen him talking to Whizziwig under the table, had she? She wasn't going to tell on him, was she? Emma was the new girl. She'd only been in his class for two weeks and already it felt as if she'd been there for years. She was a bit like a gnawing, nagging toothache you just couldn't get rid of.

'I've finished the test, sir.' Emma called out.

Mr Archer glanced up at the clock. 'Really? In only twenty minutes?'

'Yes, sir. And I'm sure my answers are all

correct! The test was easy-peasy, lemon-squeezy!'

Ben and Steve looked at each other. Others in the class started to mumble.

'Er . . . when did I say it was OK to start chatting?' Mr Archer snapped. 'The rest of you, get on with the test.'

'Would you like to check my answers, sir?' asked Emma.

Reluctantly, Mr Archer put down his book. 'OK, bring it over here and then carry on with the exercise on page seventy-five of your maths book.'

Ben finished the test and looked up at the clock. Only a few more minutes to go before everyone had to stop. He thought about telling Mr Archer that he'd finished too, but decided against it. No way did he want to be thought of as an egghead like Emma. He looked at the new girl, her nose buried in her maths workbook. She was smoothing out her eyebrows, the way she always did when she was thinking. She was very pretty. Her hair was braided in fine plaits and at the end of each one were rainbow-coloured ribbons or gold- and silver-coloured beads, decorated with tiny butterflies. She had a brace which was noticeable every time she opened her mouth, but it didn't stop her being pretty. If only she was a bit more friendly. Ben had seen Sarah and Charlotte trying to talk to her more than once, but Emma always waved them off, saying that she had to go to the library to study or to do her homework. She really was a . . . brainiac! Were books and work all she cared about? Didn't she want to make any friends? Ben turned back to his test paper to check his answers one more time. He thought he'd done OK, but it didn't hurt to check, because Mr Archer got really grouchy if he had to mark sloppy work.

Meanwhile, a few kilometres away from Ben's school, a man and a woman were in the back of a chauffeur-driven limousine – and the man was not happy. He sat stiff and upright in his seat and scowled at the woman.

'Togen, try not to look like you're about to walk the plank over crocodile-infested waters!' said the woman.

'A school visit! Franco, I can't believe you set me up with a school visit!' By now, Togen's scowl could've curdled a whole litre of fresh milk.

Franco sighed. 'It's just for an hour. It won't kill you.'

'A school visit,' Togen said with disgust. 'And why do I have to go to St Note's of all places?'

'You know why. We've been through all this before. This will be great publicity – and of the right kind for once.'

'But I don't want to go there.' Togen was sulking.

'Tough!'

'You're fired.'

Franco raised her eyebrows. 'Again? That's the third time today.'

'The more I think about it, the worse the idea gets. This is going to be a disaster – and it'll be all your fault.'

'Nonsense.' Franco sighed. 'Just smile and answer any questions thrown at you. And I've arranged for a number of reporters and photographers to turn up later for a publicity session, so behave yourself.'

'You're still fired!'

'I should be so lucky!' Franco said wistfully.

Togen leaned back into the corner of his limo for a full-blown, grade-A, top-of-the-range mega pout. Franco watched him for a few moments before leaning across to push back in his bottom lip.

'You're fired!' Togen fumed.

'Right then. Stop writing, everyone, and pass your papers to the front.' Mr Archer waited until all the test papers had arrived on his desk before he continued. 'OK, now take out your maths workbooks and turn to page . . .'

'Sir, we can't start working now,' Charlotte protested. 'Togen is coming!'

'Togen won't be here for at least another ten minutes,' Mr Archer said firmly. 'And knowing him, he'll probably be late. So we'll –'

'But, Mr Archer, aren't you *excited*?' asked Sarah. 'Togen is actually coming here, to this school. To this very classroom!'

'What's so wonderful about Togen anyway?' Ben scoffed.

Sarah gave him a pitying look. '"What's he got that I haven't?"' she said, taking the mickey. 'Nothing much, Ben. Apart from the fact that he's drop-dead gorgeous. He can sing, he can act, he plays a million instruments, he's rich . . .'

'I still don't see what all the fuss is about.' Ben sniffed.

'I quite agree, Ben,' said Mr Archer. 'Now, my . . . I mean, Togen isn't here yet and, until he is, can we please get on with some work?'

Emma put up her hand. 'Mr Archer, I've finished the two exercises on page seventy-five.'

'Already?' Mr Archer was beginning to look a bit frazzled.

'Yes, sir. Could I have some more to do?' asked Emma. 'I think I could cope with some harder ones.'

'What a crawler!' Steve whispered to Ben.

Ben nodded. 'What a swotty crawler!'

Mr Archer's head shot round at that. 'Ben! Emma works hard and she doesn't mess about. I wish you'd take a leaf out of her book!'

From within Ben's bag, Whizziwig's eyes sparkled.

'Yikes!' Ben suddenly sprang to his feet. He lurched across the classroom towards Emma, fighting against it every step of the way.

'Er, Ben? What d'you think you're doing?'

'Sir, I . . . I . . .' Before Ben could say another word, he picked up Emma's exercise book and ripped a page out.

Steve ducked down under the table. 'Whizziwig, that's not what Mr Archer meant.'

Whizziwig frowned. 'He said —'

'Never mind what he said. That's not what he meant.'

'Mr Archer, I can explain.' Ben looked from his irate teacher to the torn piece of paper in his hands and back again.

'Look what he did to my book! Just look at it!' Emma wailed. She moved her arms up and down in front of her like she was having a tantrum and bashing the air instead of the floor.

'Ben! Outside! Now!' Mr Archer roared.

Ben dragged his feet as he walked outside the classroom. How was he going to explain ripping a page out of Emma's book?

Sir, it wasn't me! An alien made me do it! Yeah, right!

Mr Archer shut the door quietly behind him before turning to Ben, his eyes practically spitting out fireworks. 'Ben, how dare you do something so spiteful?'

'I didn't mean to,' Ben mumbled.

'Nonsense. That was a deliberate act if ever I saw one. It's not like you at all. Why did you do it?'

Ben opened his mouth to defend himself, only to snap it shut again. What could he say?

'Ben, I'm waiting.' Mr Archer glared. 'Why did you tear Emma's workbook?'

'Because . . .' Ben braced himself 'Because you told me to?'

'I beg your pardon!'

'You wished I'd take a leaf out of Emma's book,' Ben tried. But from the look on Mr Archer's face, he wished he'd kept quiet.

'Don't be facetious!' The fireworks in Mr Archer's eyes had been replaced by rockets! 'Any more nonsense and you'll get detention for a week. Do I make myself clear?'

Ben nodded.

'Now, go back in and apologize,' ordered Mr Archer.

Ben walked back into the classroom, his head lowered. The moment the lesson was over, he and Whizziwig were going to have a serious talk.

'Emma, I'm sorry I ripped your book.' Ben moved to stand in front of her.

'That's OK.' Emma said grudgingly. 'I'm used to other people being jealous of me.'

'I'm not jealous of you,' Ben said at once.

'Of course you are. I'm wonderfully brilliant!' Emma shrugged.

'Get you!' Ben raised an eyebrow.

'I'm intelligent, funny, pretty, I have good taste.' Emma smiled with understanding. 'It's only natural that you'd wish you were me.'

'I'm surprised your neck doesn't crumble under the weight of your big head!' Ben told her.

'Ben, when you've quite finished,' said Mr Archer.

'But, sir, she said –'

'So?' Mr Archer interrupted. 'Emma always hands in her homework on time – with no ridiculous excuses – and it's always correct. And what's more, she's well mannered and helpful. I just wish you were a bit more like her.'

Ben stared at his teacher in horror. 'Arrgghh! Sir, take it back. Please take it back!'

'No, I won't. In fact, you'd all do well to follow Emma's example,' Mr Archer declared to the whole class. He turned back to Ben. 'Now, sit down and let's get on with the lesson.'

Ben had only just got back to his seat when the classroom door burst open. Miss Jute entered, her eyes aglow, her body a-flutter!

'Now what? Is something the matter, Miss Jute?' asked Mr Archer.

'Mr Archer, he's here! He's here!'

'Who's here?'

'Togen!' Miss Jute practically swooned. 'And he's divine!'

Before Mr Archer could say another word, Togen strutted into the room. Everyone – except Mr Archer – erupted into spontaneous applause and excitement. The sound of clapping and cheering was deafening. Mr Archer and Togen regarded each other for a few moments.

'Hi, Lennie,' said Togen.

'Hello, Martin,' Mr Archer replied.

'My name is Togen now, not Martin.' Togen stepped past Mr Archer. 'Hi, everyone. I've arrived to make your millennium.' He raised both hands and waved.

'He doesn't think much of himself, does he?' Steve said to Ben. 'He should get together with Emma.'

But at that moment, Ben had more urgent matters on his mind than a pop superstar. He ducked under his table.

'Whizzy, please tell me that you didn't grant Mr Archer's last wish.'

'I didn't grant Mr Archer's last wish,' Whizziwig told him.

Ben breathed a huge sigh of relief 'Thank

goodness for . . .' Ben ran his tongue, then his finger over the brace that had suddenly appeared on his teeth. 'Whizziwig!'

'I did grant Mr Archer's wish actually. I just thought I'd wind you up by telling you what you wanted to hear.' Whizziwig grinned.

'Great! Just great. Thanks a lot!'

'You're entirely welcome!' said Whizziwig.

'You're not going to change anything else on me, are you?' Ben pleaded.

'It's not up to me any more. I granted Mr Archer's wish, the rest is up to you and your body,' said Whizziwig.

'What does that mean?' asked Ben.

'No idea!' Whizziwig shrugged.

Stricken, Ben came out from under the table. What was he going to do? He'd just have to go home and stay in bed until the wish wore off. Goodness only knew what other parts of his body might change.

The applause in the rest of the classroom died away as everyone waited expectantly for Togen to speak.

'I've sold over five million CDs. I'm loved all over the world and I can see I'm loved just as much in this classroom,' said Togen.

Charlotte sighed with happiness. Ben frowned at her. Miss Jute sighed wistfully. Mr Archer scowled at her.

'But super-stardom has its price,' Togen carried on. 'There's a downside as well as an upside to success and fame.'

'What's the downside of selling lots of CDs and making a ton of money and being known wherever you go?' Steve was not convinced. 'Sounds great to me!'

'You think so?' said Togen. 'Well, being in the public eye all the time can seriously damage your health. That's why I've had to fork out thousands and thousands for a state-of-the-art security system for my luxury mansion. And some of my fans can be really pushy.'

'Still sounds like a cushy number to me!' Steve said.

'Yeah?' Togen frowned. 'Well, I wish you knew what it was like to be so irresistible that people never left you alone. Then maybe you'd see that it isn't all a bed of rose petals.'

Under the table, Whizziwig's eyes sparkled.

'Oh, no!' Steve gasped.

'Exactly!' said Togen.

The buzzer sounded for the end of the lesson

and the end of the school day – and not a moment too soon.

'Now, I know you've all really enjoyed yourselves.' Togen smiled. 'And the pleasure has been all yours!'

Steve grabbed his things and ran for the door. Most of the class were already on their feet.

'You'll all be wanting my autograph, of course.' Togen smiled. 'So just form a queue . . .'

'Come on, Ben. Let's go – now!' Steve urged from the door.

Ben joined Steve and they quickly left the classroom. Everyone else followed them.

'And if anyone wants to see their photo in the papers, just stay behind and I'll . . .' But Togen was wasting his breath. The classroom was empty – apart from Togen, Miss Jute, Franco and Mr Archer.

Outside in the corridor, Steve was breathing a sigh of relief.

'Hopefully, I'll get home before Togen's wish starts to kick in,' Steve told Ben.

'Never mind Togen's wish. Look at this thing in my mouth.' Ben showed Steve his brace. 'How could –'

Ben stopped speaking suddenly. He had a

strange feeling, like a prickling in the back of his neck. He turned around. So did Steve. The whole class was walking a couple of metres behind them. Ben and Steve looked at each other and tried to walk on nonchalantly, as if nothing strange was happening. They were aware that the rest of their class had started walking too. Ben and Steve stopped. So did the rest of the class. Ben and Steve looked at each other again.

'Run!' Steve yelled.

And Ben and Steve charged down the corridor, with the rest of their class racing after them.

Chapter Nineteen

Oh, Yeah!

Togen was stunned that none of the pupils in the class had stayed behind to get his autograph or tell him how wonderful he was. It was the first time something like that had ever happened. But at least Miss Jute was still looking at him like he'd invented penicillin!

'Mr Togen, can I interest you in a cup of tea in our staff room?'

Togen took Miss Jute by the arm. 'I can't think of anything I'd like more.'

Togen and Miss Jute left the classroom arm in arm. Franco watched Mr Archer seethe as he looked at Togen with his fiancée. She had to bite her lip to stop herself laughing. From the look on Mr Archer's face, Togen had better watch out.

When they reached the staff room, Miss Jute wasn't the only one who made a fuss of Togen. In the space of about fifteen seconds he was surrounded. Togen sat down, insisting that Miss Jute should sit next to him. Franco and Mr Archer found themselves being pushed back by all the other teachers. And Mr Archer's expression was getting more and more angry.

'Mr Togen, you're so funny and so talented,' Miss Jute gushed after another of Togen's jokes.

'I know!' said Togen.

Mr Archer muttered under his breath.

'I have all your CDs,' Miss Jute simpered.

Togen took hold of Miss Jute's hand and kissed it. 'Of course you do!'

Burning up with jealousy, Mr Archer stepped forward. His face was fifty different shades of purple by now.

'Your family must be so proud of you!' Miss Jute smiled.

'You think so?' Togen put an arm around Miss Jute's shoulder. 'Why don't you ask my brother whether he is or not?'

'Your brother?' Miss Jute asked, surprised.

'Lennie over there.' Togen pointed at Mr Archer.

Miss Jute's mouth fell open. 'Leonard? *Leonard* is your brother?'

'That's right. Go on, Lennie. Tell Miss Jute what you think of me,' Togen challenged.

'I think that if you don't take your hands off my fiancée, I'm going to . . . to . . .'

Togen stood up, his fists clenched. 'You're going to what?'

Mr Archer took a step forward, his jaw set. Franco watched, her arms folded across her chest. What was going to happen now?

Chapter Twenty

Changes

Ben and Steve were hiding behind a small wall in the school grounds.

'Can we go home? That crowd must've gone by now,' said Whizziwig.

Slowly, Ben and Steve raised their heads above the wall.

'I think they've . . .' Steve's voice trailed away

as he stared at Ben. 'What on earth do you look like?'

'What d'you mean?' Ben frowned.

Whizziwig floated up to get a good look at Ben. 'He looks like Emma of course.'

Appalled, Ben ran his hands over his face. 'What's the matter? Whizziwig, what've you done?'

Ben ran his hands over his head. Where he'd had short, neat hair before, he now had . . . plaits. Short plaits springing out from all over, with the odd bead and bauble and ribbon dotted at the end of some of them.

'No!' Ben wailed. 'Whizziwig, take them off! At once.'

'Can't do that. Sorry! Besides, they rather suit you. They give you a –'

'There they are!' shouted a voice from across the school grounds.

Ben and Steve turned their heads to see the rest of the class racing towards them.

'Run!' Steve yelled.

And Ben didn't need to be told twice.

Meanwhile, back in the staff room, Mr Archer and Togen were squaring up to each other.

'You haven't changed,' Togen sneered. 'Still the same old pompous, bossy big brother.'

'And you haven't changed either,' said Mr Archer furiously. 'Still the same old irresponsible half-wit who thinks he just has to smile to get away with murder.'

'Oh, yeah?'

'Yeah!'

'Oh, yeah?' Togen pushed his brother's shoulder.

'Yes, yeah!' Mr Archer pushed him back. 'How many more times?'

'Mr Togen! Leonard! Please,' Miss Jute tried – but in vain.

Togen and Mr Archer carried on pushing each other, and every push was getting harder. Until they grabbed each other and fell to the floor. Fists flew in all directions as each brother tried to get the upper hand.

'Someone do something. Leonard! Togen! Please stop.' Miss Jute ran over to Franco. 'Miss Franco, do something!'

'My name isn't Miss Franco, or even Franco. It's Frances,' Franco said calmly.

'But I heard Mr Togen call you . . .'

'That's just one of my husband's feeble little

116

jokes.' Franco sighed.

'Togen's your *husband*?' Miss Jute said, astounded.

Franco watched Togen and Mr Archer scuffle about on the ground. 'Yes – unfortunately.'

'Do something!' Miss Jute pleaded.

'OK. A fiver on Leonard Archer! Any takers?'

Some of the other teachers gathered around to take up the bet.

'Frances, that's not the something I had in mind. Stop them.' Miss Jute was beginning to wonder if she was speaking another language. Was she really the only one concerned about what was going on in the staff room?

'I'm not going to stop them. It would serve my husband right if your fiancé wiped the floor with him,' said Franco.

Miss Jute gave up. Franco was absolutely no use at all.

'You stay away from Judy, d'you understand? She's worth fifty of you!' Mr Archer sat on his brother's chest to stop him from getting up. But then Togen reared up like a bucking mule and once again he and Mr Archer were rolling on the floor.

At that precise moment, the staff-room door opened. Reporters and photo journalists strolled into the room. And the moment they saw what was going on, their cameras started flashing. Mr Archer and Togen looked up from the floor to see what all the lights were. Mr Archer watched appalled as yet more flash photos were taken. He sprang to his feet, but it was too late.

Chapter Twenty-one

Disguises

Ben and Steve stood panting outside Ben's front door. They'd run all the way from school and the crowd were still chasing behind them. Panic-stricken, Steve urged, 'Come on, Ben, before they tear me limb from limb.'

'STEVE! STEVE!' the crowd behind them chanted.

'Can I have a kiss, Steve?'

'Can I have your autograph?'

'Steve, can I have your shirt?'

The cries of the mob were getting closer and closer.

In his hurry to get his key in the lock, Ben dropped it on the ground. He dived after it, the beads at the end of his plaits swinging into his face.

'I've got to do something about my hair,' he muttered.

'NEVER MIND YOUR HAIR. OPEN THE DOOR,' Steve yelled.

Ben scrambled to his feet and pushed the key into the lock. The mob were almost at the front gate.

'BEN!' Steve shouted

The door flew open. Steve and Ben dived into the hall. Steve kicked the door shut behind him, just as the mob were coming up the front path.

Whizziwig floated out of Ben's bag. 'If that's what it's like to be famous, then I must say I'm not keen.'

'Why do these things always happen to me?' Ben gasped, trying to catch his breath.

'Especially when I'm so extra-wonderfully brilliant. Not to mention talented!'

'My whole life flashed before my eyes there.' Steve moved away from the front door. 'I was terrified.'

'First things first,' Ben announced, standing up. 'I've got to do something about my hair. And with that he strode off to the bathroom.

Outside, it'd suddenly gone quiet. Steve crept back to the front door and peeped through the letter box. The crowd were standing outside the front gate on the pavement. They were looking up at the house. Steve moved back quickly, but he was too late. He'd been spotted.

'WE WANT STEVE! WE WANT STEVE!'

'I wouldn't do that if I were you,' said Whizziwig.

'Don't worry! I'm not going to do it again.' Steve shook his head and went off to find Ben.

Ben was in the bathroom, cutting off first one plait, then another and another. He threw each of them into the bin so hard that they bounced.

'So much for my plaits and flowery beads!' he said as he threw the last braid in.

'I wish my problem was as easy to solve.' Steve sighed.

'I can't grant that. You wished for yourself –' Whizziwig began.

'I know that,' Steve said, annoyed.

He and Whizziwig left the bathroom first, followed by Ben.

'How does Emma cope with this brace?' Ben ran his tongue over it. 'I feel like I've got a hanger in my mouth!'

'Never mind your brace,' said Steve. 'Or your plaits. I need your help.'

'What plaits?' Ben's hands flew to his head. The plaits were back, and even longer than before.

'Oh, no!'

'Ben . . .' Steve began.

But Whizziwig had Ben's full attention. 'Whizziwig, *please* get rid of these things. I'll do whatever you say. I'll never make another wish again. Just get rid of them.'

'No can do, I'm afraid. You'll just have to wait until tomorrow.'

'You're useless,' Ben hissed.

'And you're charming!' smiled Whizziwig.

'Ben, I –' Steve tried.

'At least tomorrow is Saturday,' Ben interrupted Steve. 'So that's something. Whizzy, tell me that's it! Tell me you're not going to change any other part of my body.'

'I must confess, I'm not quite sure how this wish is going to work,' Whizziwig admitted

'Ben, I –'

But Steve was interrupted again.

'Whizziwig, what're my mum and dad going to say if I turn into a girl? How am I going to explain that?'

'BEN!' Steve had had enough.

'What's the matter?' Ben replied crossly. 'And by the way, that shirt doesn't go with those trousers. Blue and green should not be seen! A tulip-red or a nice purple shirt would look a lot better.'

'Ben, get a grip!' Steve ordered.

'Sorry!' Ben said ruefully. 'What's the problem?'

'How am I going to get home?'

'Have your legs stopped working?' Whizziwig asked.

'In case you hadn't noticed, there's a mob outside who won't let me leave this house – not alive, at any rate!' said Steve.

'Hmmm!' Ben smoothed out his eyebrows as he had a think. 'I've got it! Come with me!'

Ben and Steve raced up the stairs, with Whizziwig floating along behind them. Ben led the way into his mum and dad's bedroom. He sat Steve down in front of the dressing table and searched through his mum's wardrobe.

'Found it!' Ben grinned.

And before Steve could stop him, he put the golden-brown wig in his hands on Steve's head.

'No way! You must be joking!' Steve tried to pull it off, but Ben wouldn't let him.

'D'you want to leave this house today or not?' Ben asked him.

'I'm not wearing this wig,' Steve insisted.

'In that case, I'll be sure to visit you in hospital once your fans outside have finished with you,' said Ben.

Steve's hands dropped to his side. 'Whizziwig, this is all your fault!'

'Don't look at me.' Whizziwig sniffed. 'You're the one who kept going on about how wonderful it must be to be famous.'

'I take it all back,' Steve said at once. He looked at his reflection and shook his head.

'How come your mum wears a wig then? Or is it your dad's?'

'No, it is not my dad's,' Ben said with indignation. 'Mum wore it to a fancy-dress party she went to a while ago.'

'What did she go as? A muppet?' asked Steve.

'No, she did not! She was Tina Turner.'

'D'you think this will work?' Steve said doubtfully.

Ben stroked his eyebrows for a moment.

'Of course it will work. I thought of it and I'm extra-wonderfully brilliant.' He smiled. 'I've considered your problem from every angle and this is the best solution. Besides, I'm never wrong about these things.'

'You've certainly got Emma's modesty,' Steve said. 'OK, Ben, I trust you. I just wish I didn't look so ridiculous.'

'Try wearing beads with butterflies and flowers on them some time,' Ben replied.

'So now what?' interrupted Steve.

'Now we make sure that no one outside can possibly recognize you.' Ben smiled. 'I've got it all worked out ... At least I think I have!'

'Ben ...'

'It'll be all right . . . At least I think it will!' Ben frowned.

'If you're not sure . . .' Steve was looking very worried now.

'It's just that it takes a lot of thought and energy to be right all the time. I'm just trying to make sure I haven't overlooked anything. OK?'

'I don't like the sound of this,' Steve said.

'But you don't have much choice, do you?' Whizziwig pointed out.

And Steve couldn't argue with that.

Chapter Twenty-two

The Great Escape

Two heads popped up from the side wall of Ben's back garden. One was covered with ribbons and beads. The other wore a Tina Turner wig. Ben was still wearing his brace and he was sure he could feel his eyelashes growing with each passing moment. Steve wore Ben's mum's blue flowery dress over his own clothes.

The dress was belted in the middle to make sure that it stayed in place.

'Quick! Over the wall while the coast is clear,' Ben whispered.

They both clambered over the wall and on to the pavement.

'I swear if you ever tell anyone about this . . .' Steve began.

'You must be joking. I'm not going to tell anyone,' Ben replied at once. He looked around. Further down the road towards the front of his house, he saw two girls in the crowd watching them. He quickly turned away. 'We're being watched,' he warned Steve.

Steve began to turn around.

'NO! Don't look at them. Just start walking away,' Ben urged.

Steve started to stride off in the opposite direction.

'No, walk slowly,' said Ben. 'Walk like a girl!'

Ben started walking with a very peculiar sway to show Steve how to do it.

'No way am I going to walk like that. There are limits, you know!' said Steve.

Ben and Steve started walking up the road. They didn't notice the limousine driving past them. Inside, Franco sat next to Togen. She smiled maliciously as she dabbed at his swollen eye, his cut lip and his sore hand.

'Does it hurt?' she asked with a grin.

''Course it hurts!' Togen snapped.

'Isn't that a shame!' Franco's grin broadened. 'Maybe next time you'll behave yourself.'

'Yeah! You look totally devastated!' Togen glanced out of the window and saw the crowd outside Ben's house. 'Stop the car! Stop the car!'

Franco looked through the car window at the crowd and raised her eyes heavenwards. She knew what was coming next. Togen pressed a button and the window in the car door beside him moved down silently. He leaned out.

'Hi, everyone!'

All heads in the crowd turned to face him.

'Yes, it's me.' Togen smiled. 'Anyone want my autograph?'

Every head turned back to Ben's house.

'We want Steve! We want Steve!' the crowd chanted.

Togen's lips quivered at the rejection. Franco gathered up Togen for a cuddle as he turned to sob on her shoulder.

'There! There!' she told him, patting his head. 'I still love you!'

And the limousine drove on.

Ben and Steve dared to breathe a sigh of relief only once they'd turned the corner and the crowd were no longer in sight.

'Right! You should be OK from here if you go straight home,' Ben said.

'Aren't you going to come with me?'

'Not on your life! No one will recognize you. But I've got these horrible butterfly beads in my hair and the plaits don't even look like boys' plaits – they look like girls' plaits. I'm not walking down the street like this.'

'Aren't you two going to thank me?' asked Whizziwig.

'Thank you for what?' Ben frowned.

'Well, you've both never looked lovelier!' Whizziwig grinned.

It was hard to say whose expression was more icy, Ben's or Steve's.

'You want to watch that sense of humour of yours, Whizziwig. It might get you accidentally sat on or something!' Steve told her.

'I won't say another word.' Whizziwig mimed zipping up her lips.

'Very wise,' Ben told her. 'And if any other part of my body changes, Whizziwig, I'll never let you hear the end of it. I'm going to have to pretend to be ill and stay in bed all day tomorrow as it is.'

Whizziwig looked dismayed. 'But I thought that tomorrow we were all going to the –'

'Neither of us is setting a foot outside until these wishes have worn off,' Steve interrupted.

'I don't understand why you're both so scared to be seen. You look drop-dead gorgeous!'

Ben had had enough. He shut his bag decisively.

'Ooof. Watch it!' a muffled Whizziwig complained.

'I'll see you on Monday morning!' said Steve.

'OK. See you then.'

Ben and Steve turned to go their separate ways. Moments later, Ben turned around.

'Steve?'

Steve turned back to face Ben.

'Can I have your autograph?'

'You're not funny!' Steve fumed.

'A lock of your hair then?' Ben grinned.

'You're still not funny.' Steve marched off, very annoyed.

Chapter Twenty-three

Results

First thing on Monday morning, Ben entered the classroom and looked around. There were no girls-only beads and ribbons in his hair and the brace had gone. He was himself again. Steve wasn't in the classroom yet, but Emma was. After a moment's thought, Ben walked over to her.

'Hi, Emma.'

'Hello, Ben.' Emma nodded. She returned to the book on her desk.

'What're you doing?'

'Just checking through my homework,' Emma replied.

'Why?' asked Ben. 'It's bound to be right.'

'I just thought I'd make sure.' Emma didn't look up. She carried on scrutinizing her homework.

'It's hard work, isn't it?' Ben said after a few moments.

'What is?' Emma asked, looking up.

'Being good at things, knowing things. Now Mr Archer and everyone else expects you to be right all the time. You probably don't have time to do anything else but work and study to make sure you don't slip.'

'It was the same at my last school.' Emma looked at Ben, really looked at him. Then she sighed. 'D'you know, you're the first person who's understood.'

'I sort of put myself in your place – or rather, Mr Archer did!' Ben smiled.

'Pardon?'

'It doesn't matter.' Ben shook his head.

'Listen! You don't have to know every single fact in the universe.'

'Don't I?' Emma sighed again.

Charlotte and Sarah, who'd been listening, wandered over.

'No, you don't.'

'But everyone expects me to.' Emma's voice had dropped, but she could still be heard.

'Rubbish!' said Sarah. 'You're harder on yourself than anyone else could be.'

'You need to enjoy yourself a bit more,' Charlotte told her.

'I don't know . . .' Emma began.

'Sarah's coming over to my house after school for tea. Would you like to come?' asked Charlotte.

'I don't . . . er . . .'

'It'll be fun,' Charlotte insisted.

Emma looked down at her homework, then closed her exercise book. 'Yes, OK! I'd love to come!'

'Great!' Sarah grinned.

'Can I come too?' Ben asked.

'No!' Charlotte, Sarah and Emma all spoke at once.

'I get the message,' said Ben drily and he walked back to his seat.

*

Mr Archer entered the staff room. The skin around his left eye was a gruesome shade of purple. The moment the other teachers spotted him, they all stood up and started clapping. Mr Archer was horribly embarrassed. He tried to hide his face behind his briefcase but Mrs Jenkins held a Sunday newspaper under his nose. The headline read: BROTHERLY LOVE. TOGEN AT IT AGAIN. And beside it was a picture of Mr Archer and Togen rolling about on the floor. Mr Archer groaned. Miss Jute rushed over to him.

'Oh, Leonard! How are you?'

'Fine, Judy. Fine.' Mr Archer mumbled. How he wished the other teachers would all stop clapping and sit down.

'It wasn't a very good example to set for your class, was it?'

'No, it wasn't,' Mr Archer agreed humbly.

'But you were quite dashing – in a yobbo hooligan fashion!' said Miss Jute.

'I'm so sorry, Judy. I'll never be able to live this down. I can't think what came over me,' Mr Archer said unhappily.

'I think I can.' Miss Jute smiled.

Mr Archer looked at her and smiled back.

'Never mind, Leonard. I've got just the thing to cheer you up.' Miss Jute dug into her handbag. 'How about dinner for two tonight, followed by a concert?'

'A concert?' Mr Archer looked more happy already. 'Sounds wonderful! Is it Mozart? Or Brahms?'

Miss Jute glanced down at the two tickets in her handbag. They had TOGEN IN CONCERT emblazoned across them. She decided to leave them in her handbag until the last possible moment.

'It's a surprise!' she told Mr Archer. 'And you'll love it!'

Steve entered the classroom, carrying a dark carrier bag. He headed straight for Ben.

'Hi, Steve. How come you didn't knock for me this morning?' Ben asked.

'It'll be a while before I can pluck up the courage to go anywhere near your house,' Steve admitted.

'Why?'

'Too many painful memories!' said Steve. He handed Ben the carrier bag. 'These belong to you – or rather your mum. Did she miss them?'

'No.' Ben couldn't resist adding, 'And anyway, I'm sure she'd let you keep them if you really wanted to!'

'You're still not funny,' Steve replied. 'I'll show you what I really want to do with them.'

Steve dropped the carrier bag on the ground and started jumping up and down on it.

'Hang on, Steve. I've still got the last set of plaits I cut off,' said Ben. He dug into his bag. 'Excuse me, Whizziwig.'

'Don't mind me,' said Whizziwig.

Ben took out some plaits with beads and ribbons attached to their ends and dropped them on to the floor next to Steve's carrier bag. Then he joined with Steve in jumping up and down on them.

'Hmmm!' Whizziwig said from beneath Ben's table. 'I obviously still have a lot to learn about humans!'